DOMHNALL'S HONOR

HIGHLANDER FATE, LAIRDS OF THE ISLES
BOOK THREE

STELLA KNIGHT

PRONUNCIATION GUIDE

Domhnall - DOH-nuhl
Ruarc - RORK
Siomha - SHEE-vuh
Neacal - NIY-kl
Moirna - MOY-er-nuh
Fyfa - FEE-fuh
Lachina - Lock-EEN-ah
Ulf - OOLF
Aodh - AY
Erskina - ERSK-in-uh

CHAPTER 1

1266

Leagh Isle, Scottish Isles

A thick layer of fog hovered over Leagh Isle as Domhnall trudged toward the fishing cottage that clung to the edge of one of the ragged cliffs that lined the coast. He could barely make out the features of the isle that surrounded him—the cliffs, the rugged yet verdant glens, even the churning waters of the surrounding ocean, though he could taste the salt in the air.

He knew the fog would lift come midday, when the sun's rays fought their way past its impenetrable cover, but he couldn't help but feel a sense of foreboding as he approached the doorway of the cottage. The tension that coiled around his belly tightened like a noose, and he expelled a breath.

Ye're doing this for yer people. Yer clan, he told himself, as a wave of guilt washed over him at the prospect of what he was about to do.

He forced himself to enter the cottage.

Inside, his cousin Ulf stood with his back to him, warming his hands by the fire that roared in the central hearth. Ulf turned, his eyes lighting up at the sight of him. Domhnall returned his smile, hoping his inner turmoil didn't show as an array of emotions roiled through him; dread, unease, fear.

Ulf strode across the room, reaching out to clap him on the shoulder.

"Cousin," Ulf said. "It's good to see you well."

Ulf's warm greeting only increased Domhnall's guilt, but he made himself nod.

He took in Ulf; he'd last seen him two Yules ago. He and his cousin shared the same blond hair and ice-blue eyes that told of their Norse ancestry. Their manner of speech was the biggest distinction between them; Domhnall's tongue displayed the Gaelic side of his bloodline that he lived and breathed, while Ulf's brogue was fully Norse, the side that he fully embraced.

"You are well, cousin?" Ulf pressed, his smile fading as he took in Domhnall's tight expression.

"Aye," Domhnall said, forcing the tension from his expression and giving his cousin a smile. "And ye?"

"The sea was rough getting here, but it was worth the journey to see my cousin—to discuss what must be discussed in person and not by letter or messenger."

Ulf turned, looking around the small cottage, shaking his head as a look of nostalgia entered his eyes.

"I still remember the last time we were here as lads," he said. "Remember Uncle Svend? What a terrible fisherman he was. He would be in a mood whenever he didn't catch fish—which was often."

Domhnall couldn't help but smile at the memory of his Uncle Svend, who was indeed a terrible, moody fisherman. But his smile faded. Svend was yet another reminder of the blood ties he shared with Ulf.

Ulf gestured to a table where a large jug of ale sat. Domhnall took a seat, hoping that his visage appeared neutral and relaxed.

"Have you thought about my proposal, cousin?" Ulf asked, his tone becoming serious.

'Tis all I've been able tae think about.

"Aye," Domhnall said, forcing himself to hold his cousin's gaze as he spoke the next words, words which were lies. "And I agree with it."

Stark relief passed over Ulf's face as he sat, offering Domhnall a wide grin.

"I was afraid you wouldn't," Ulf said. "I was afraid you'd let your men sway you into betraying your own blood."

They're my blood as well, Domhnall wanted to shout.

Ulf and Domhnall shared blood on their mother's side; Ulf was the son of his maternal uncle. Domhnall ruled lands on the Isle of Barra, an isle where the descendants of the great Somerled, a Norse-Gael, had long ruled. But ever since the Norse king had signed a peace treaty with the Scottish king over the contested isles between Scotland and Norway, Barra and other isles that had once belonged to the Norse, now belonged to Scotland.

While the Scottish king left the isles of Somerled to remain self-governed under the native clans, they had become more and more Gaelicized, and the Norse knew it.

Including his cousin.

Domhnall had only known life on the isle he had inherited through his father's side, a proud Norse-Gael descended from both the Norse and Gaelic kings. Barra was his home, and he was loyal to it, his clan, and the people who resided there. He loved Ulf and his Norse kin, but he would do whatever it took to protect his home . . . even if it meant betraying his cousin, who wanted to ignore the treaty and take back the isles for the Norse. He had tried, without success, to dissuade Ulf from his intentions, but his cousin had only grown more determined.

He ultimately had no choice but to pretend to agree with Ulf's plan, all the while supplying information to his own men, information that could impede his cousin. He knew what he was doing was for the greater good, but that didn't stop the guilt that continually raged within him.

"I always knew the king was a weakling. To give up the isles—lands that are ours by right," Ulf was saying, anger flaring in his blue eyes. "We will take them back—damn what the treaty says."

"Aye," Domhnall murmured in agreement, though his stomach churned.

"I know it will be difficult to go against your men. But they will soon understand that the isles are ours—and they were, long before the Scots made a claim."

Domhnall studied his cousin, whose eyes were now alight with greed, wondering where the kind lad he'd grown up with had gone. What had led to this greed? How could Domhnall have stopped it?

"Are ye nae happy with yer lands on Orkney?" Domhnall asked, before he could stop himself. The Norse still held the Shetlands and Orkney, and Domhnall, along with his Scottish allies, had hoped those lands would appease them.

Ulf stiffened at his words, his eyes going dark, and Domhnall knew he had asked the wrong question.

"No. I want my ancestral home, the one taken from me by the Scots and their king."

Ulf leaned back in his chair, staring at Domhnall with narrowed eyes.

"You're not turning your back on your blood, are you?"

Panic surged in Domhnall's belly; he couldn't have Ulf suspecting him.

"Nae," Domhnall said, fixing him with a glare

that he hoped was convincing. "Donnae accuse me of such a thing."

A silence laced with tension stretched between them for several long moments until Ulf broke it. "I apologize, cousin," Ulf said finally, his glare giving way to an apologetic smile. "I know you'll never betray me."

Domhnall's guilt once again roared to life, but he steadily held his cousin's gaze.

"Now," Ulf said, leaning forward, "we discuss how we take our lands back from the Scots."

DOMHNALL WAVED FAREWELL TO ULF, who stood on the shore of Leagh as Domhnall's men guided his boat away from the isle. He only turned away when his cousin became a speck on the horizon, facing the churning waters of the ocean as his boat made its way back to Barra.

His father had once told him that despite how violent the ocean could become, it was the most peaceful place a man could be. Their people, the old Gaels, were people of the ocean who had settled the isles that surrounded them, learning to coexist and make peace with the great waters. His mother had told him similar tales of her Norse ancestors, how they had always felt more at home at sea. Love of the ocean and seafaring linked the two sides of his bloodline.

He was the only child of his parents, whom

he'd loved fiercely. His mother had died long ago when he was still a lad, his father only years ago, leaving him as chief of their clan and laird of Farraige Castle, but he still thought of them often. What would they think of his betrayal of his cousin? Would they be proud? Disappointed? Both?

"Leadership is nae an easy path, son," his father had told him on his deathbed. "No decision will come easy, none will feel right. I still donnae ken if I made the right decision about events long since passed."

"Then how do ye ever ken ye've made the right decision?" Domhnall had asked.

His father had only given him a sad smile. "That's the thing, my son. Ye never do."

The shouts of his men pulled him from thoughts of the past as their boat neared the shore of Barra. He followed their gazes, stiffening with surprise.

A lass lay sprawled out on the shore, eerily still.

CHAPTER 2

*A*t first, Astrid only felt—and heard.

The dampness of sand on her flesh. The scent of salty ocean in the air. The crisp breeze against her skin. The crashing of waves on a shore.

And then shouts. Masculine shouts.

She opened her eyes to find herself lying prone on a beach, and for several tense seconds she forgot how she'd gotten there . . . until it all came back to her.

Visions of the past in her own time, visions that had driven her to use her magical ability to travel back through time. Magic she'd long turned her back on.

Arriving in Scotland and then driving to the fairy pools of Skye. The array of images she'd seen on the surface of the waters. The fateful leap she'd taken into the water—the leap that pulled her back through time.

She sat up, shivering and terrified, turning to

face the direction of the shouts. A group of about a half-dozen men approached her, wearing belted tunics with swords at their hilts.

"Oh my God . . ." she whispered.

Her hands flew to her mouth as icy fear skated through her, the full implication of where she was hitting her with the force of a ton of bricks. Unless those men were playing an elaborate prank on her, their clothing proved that she was indeed in the past. She'd traveled back in time from the relative security of the twenty-first century to the dangerous past. A past where a woman alone wasn't safe.

And the men approaching her were regarding her with suspicion.

Another jolt of fear tore through her as she scrambled to her feet, her heart hammering. Had they seen her appear here—out of nowhere? If so, they'd suspect—*know*—she was a witch, and she knew what people did to witches in this time.

As the men drew near, she instinctively held out her hands, trying to think of a spell—any spell— that could protect her. But her magic was rusty, and though she'd practiced a few Defensive spells before she'd left the present, fear made all of her senses, and her magical ability, go into freeze mode.

One of the men, who she assumed was the leader, turned to order the other men back in words she couldn't hear. The men hung back but continued to regard her with suspicion.

The leader drew closer, his hands held up in a gesture of appeasement.

Her heart leapt into her throat. She recognized him. It was the man she'd seen in her visions, in her dreams, even in the waters in the fairy pools of Skye before she'd taken that fateful leap.

But the visions didn't do him justice in the flesh; she wasn't prepared for the physical affect he had on her. His muscular form towered over her at six and a half feet, with wavy blond hair that came nearly to his shoulders, ice-blue eyes and a dusting of beard along his strong jawline. A proud, aristocratic nose along with a wide, sensual mouth only enhanced his masculinity.

Her breath hitched in her throat and her mouth went dry, her already accelerated heartbeat increasing its thunderous pace in her chest. Hot desire chased away her fear, along with a certain calm, a deep-seated knowledge that somehow, she was safe with this man.

Yet her sense of safety with him made no sense. Other than in her visions, she'd never seen him before. Still, she couldn't get past the sense that she knew this man somehow. That she was *meant* to know this man.

"I'll nae hurt ye, lass."

Astrid jerked in surprise. The man looked like a Viking but had the voice of a Highlander, his thick accent shaping his words in an odd manner she'd never heard before. It bore some similarities to the modern Scottish brogue but was far more difficult to understand, with harsher consonants and vowels.

The man kept his hands up, his eyes warm, but they held traces of suspicion.

"How did ye come tae be here? Where is yer escort? Yer ship?"

It took some time to wrap her mind around what he was saying, and when it did, panic seized her. She hadn't thought through what she'd do once she arrived here. She'd naïvely assumed she'd have more time to prepare once she arrived in the past. How could she have known she'd run into the man from her visions so abruptly?

She couldn't just tell the man she'd traveled through time, could she? Her coven leader, Siobhan, had told her that there were some who were aware of witches and magic in the past, but most were not, believing it was evil if such a thing existed.

She was just going to pray that Domhnall was aware of witches, but was in the minority who didn't think they were evil. Only she couldn't tell him who she really was now. Not with his suspicious men hovering behind him.

Say something, Astrid. Anything, she thought frantically. She shivered as the ocean breeze battered her body and wrapped her arms around herself. The man's handsome features tightened, but not with anger—with protectiveness.

"Did someone harm ye, lass?" he practically growled. "Is that what has ye frightened so?"

Without thinking, she gave him a jerky nod. His face remained tight, and he turned to shout something to the other men. They nodded and scattered. He took another step toward her, still keeping his hands up.

"I'm Laird Domhnall Flachnan, chieftain of the Flachnan clan of Barra," he said gently. "Ye're on my lands, and ye're now under my protection."

Domhnall Flachnan. Again, that tug of familiarity pulled at her. But she was certain she'd never heard the name before.

"Can ye walk, lass? I'll take ye back tae my castle where ye can have a hot broth and change intae warm clothes. I can protect ye from whoever caused ye harm."

She gave him another jerky nod, but as soon as she stepped forward, her legs wobbled. He immediately moved forward and swept her up into his arms. The reaction of her body was instant—a heated awareness that went right to her center. A firestorm of electricity flared throughout her entire body.

"I've got ye, lass," he murmured. "Ye're safe with me."

And even though she was hundreds of years in the past, thousands of miles from home, she believed him.

~

ASTRID SAT on Domhnall's horse, his muscular arms wrapped around her, as they approached a causeway that led to an honest-to-goodness, straight-out-of-a-medieval-fairytale castle. It sat perched on a rocky islet linked to Barra by the causeway, its gray stone towers gleaming in the sunlight. In her time, most castles were in ruins; to see such a striking castle in its heyday was . . . surreal.

Astrid tried to calm her reaction to Domhnall's touch as they neared the castle; she'd spent the brief journey from the beach to the castle trying to come up with what she was going to say, but it had proved difficult with Domhnall's muscular arms wrapped around her. He hadn't spoken to her during the journey, for which she was grateful. It gave her much-needed time to think. If, for whatever reason, her instincts were wrong, and he had her thrown into the dungeons for being a witch, she needed an escape plan.

"Ye'll be safe here, lass."

Domhnall's husky voice catapulted her from her thoughts, close against her ear, and another jolt of desire shot through her.

She gritted her teeth with frustration. If she was going to stay in this time and do whatever her magic needed her to do, she needed to quell her off-the-charts attraction to this man.

They entered a bustling courtyard where Domhnall dismounted, reaching up to help her down. Despite her resolve to calm her reactions toward him, a shiver roiled through her at his touch. His hands seemed to linger on her waist before he abruptly stepped back.

"Follow me," he said gruffly.

She obeyed, trailing him through the courtyard and into the castle. The inside of the castle was even larger than it appeared from the outside, with cavernous corridors, stone walls hung with tapestries, all lit by flickering candlelight. It was a hubbub of activity, filled with dozens of servants dressed in simple tunics moving to and fro around her. Most of them were shorter than people in her own time, Astrid herself taller than most of them, which made Domhnall's height even more impressive.

Domhnall led her through the winding corridors to a large, bustling kitchen, where even more servants were milling about—hauling in buckets of water, grinding flour, scrubbing down floors, chopping heaps of vegetables. Many of them stopped working at the sight of Domhnall, straightening with respect as he approached.

A petite, elderly woman stepped forward with a frown, setting down a rag and rubbing her hands on her apron.

"My laird?" she asked, her gaze sweeping to Astrid with confusion. "Is this a new maid?"

"No. This lass is my personal guest who is under my protection. Find her a chamber, feed her, and get her some warm clothes."

"Aye, my laird," the woman said instantly.

Domhnall turned to her, giving her a smile that made her insides melt.

"Saibhe will take care of ye. I'll come tae see ye later."

Unease spiraled through her at the notion of being separated from him and on her own. She'd only been in this time for a matter of minutes, yet Domhnall already felt like an anchor. He seemed to sense her unease and gave her a reassuring smile.

"Ye're safe here. Ye have my word," he said.

His words reassured her, and she gave him a nod.

"Ye need nae be afeared," Saibhe said moments later, giving her a reassuring smile of her own as she led Astrid into a sprawling chamber complete with a massive bed, fireplace, and windows that looked out onto the waters surrounding the castle. "The laird is a good man. He will protect ye from whoever has done ye harm."

Guilt pierced Astrid; they assumed she was some sort of victim and she hadn't corrected them. But in a way, wasn't she a victim of the magic she didn't want? Magic that had compelled her to travel back to the past by torturing her with dark visions?

Astrid merely nodded and Saibhe left her with another patient smile. Only moments later, a young chambermaid entered her room with a wooden bath, a hot broth, and a gown for her to change into. Saibhe left her and the chambermaid alone, and Astrid realized in horror the maid was here to help her bathe.

She almost opened her mouth to protest but didn't want to give away her modern accent. *This is a different time, whatever year this is,* she reminded herself. *You have to go along with the different things people did.*

The maid's accent was even stronger than Saibhe's and Domhnall's, and Astrid had to concentrate to understand her as she helped her into the bath. The maid's eyes widened with surprise at her smooth, unmarked skin.

Astrid was a doctor in her own time, but even if she weren't, she knew that her unmarked skin wasn't common in the past, in a time before modern medicine and vaccines. She could only pray that the chambermaid wouldn't gossip; she didn't want to stand out.

The maid said nothing and dutifully washed her, helping her into a white linen underdress and a high-waisted dark blue gown before leaving her.

Once she was alone, Astrid moved over to sit by the fireplace, drinking the surprisingly flavorful hot broth as she gazed into leaping flames of the fireplace. Her heart was still racing at about a thousand miles per hour, and though she knew she was in the past, she still felt as if she were suspended in a dream from which she'd soon wake.

But everyone she'd seen and spoken to was very real, including the devastatingly gorgeous Domhnall.

Just tell him the truth. The sooner and more forthright she was with him, the sooner she could get to the business of obeying her magic and helping him, and then returning to her own time.

She thought she would have hours to prepare what she was going to say, but it wasn't long until Domhnall entered her chamber. A flood of emotions enveloped her at the sight of him—that nagging familiarity, nervousness, and the undeniable pull of desire.

He approached her with a concerned frown. "Are ye well, lass?" he asked.

She nodded, getting to her feet on shaky legs.

"I never asked yer name," he continued, offering a kind smile, making his handsome features even more so.

She returned his smile and stood, expelling a breath. It was now or never.

"My name is Astrid," she said, watching his eyes widen at her strange manner of speech. "Domhnall . . . you're the reason I'm here."

CHAPTER 3

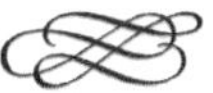

*I*t took several long moments for Astrid's words to register. When they did, Domhnall just stared at her in disbelief, certain that he hadn't heard her correctly.

"Have—have you heard of the stiuireadh?" she pressed in that strange accent of hers.

He stiffened, drawing himself up to his full height. Aye, he had heard of the stiuireadh, but he had also heard of the sidhe and other mythical creatures that children and superstitious old women believed in.

"I'm a stiuireadh, from a time yet to come," Astrid continued in a rush. "I've had visions of you, and I know you need my help. Something is coming, something dark that threatens you and the people here. I don't know exactly what it is, I just know that my magic—that time itself—wanted me to come here to help you . . . whatever year this is. What—what year is it?"

Domhnall's astonishment and disbelief faded, replaced by a growing anger as the sheer nonsense of her words settled in. It had been difficult to understand her words with her accent, and what he had understood made no sense. She had come from a time yet to come? She didn't know what year it was? She had *visions*? And she claimed to be a stiuireadh, a witch who could perform magic? He'd always thought that if such creatures did exist, they would look like just that—creatures. But Astrid just looked like a regular lass. An exceedingly bonnie one, but a lass nonetheless.

He stared at her, searching her expression for any hint of malfeasance, of deceit. But she was looking at him with clear, albeit desperate, eyes.

His anger spiked, and he took a step back from her. She must be a spy, sent to him by the Norse, or perhaps by another clan, to seduce him, pry information out of him. His eyes raked over her; the tumble of dark curls that cascaded past her shoulders, the luminescent green eyes, the soft beauty of her features, her tempting curves. It would explain why she was so damned desirable. Had his cousin sent her, having guessed his true intentions?

"Who sent ye?" he growled.

She blinked at him, looking genuinely astonished.

"Wh—what?"

"Who. Sent. Ye?"

"N—no one. I mean, my magic," she stammered, flushing as she seemed to realize how absurd that must sound. "I saw visions of you, and—"

"Stop yer lies," he hissed. "Aye, I've heard of the stiuireadh, but I ken they're creatures of fancy. They donnae exist. Who are ye in truth?"

"I'm telling you the truth!" she cried, her voice rising with desperation. "My name is Astrid. Astrid Hart. I'm not sure what century this is, but I'm from the twenty-first century. I came here through the fairy pools in Skye, a portal. Not only have I had visions of you, but I saw you in the waters there, and—"

"Enough," he snapped.

The twenty-first century? He couldn't fathom such a distant time. And visions of him in waters? Was the lass mad?

Yet Astrid was looking at him with urgent desperation, clearly determined to stick to her lies. She licked her dry lips with her tongue, and he hated the shard of desire that stabbed him at the sight. He averted his gaze, cursing himself for his foolishness, for that overwhelming sense of protectiveness, and heated desire, that had washed over him when he'd come across her on the shore.

"I'll give ye the rest of the day tae tell me the truth. Ye'll stay in this chamber for now, but if ye persist in yer lies, I'll put ye in the dungeons until ye tell me the truth."

When he looked at her again, anger had filled her green eyes; anger and fear, which he tried to not let affect him. She reached out to grip his arm, her touch sending a rush of heat racing through him.

"Domhnall, I'm telling you the truth, I swear. Why—why do you think I sound so strange? Have you ever heard an accent like mine? How do you think I arrived on that shore without an escort—no horse, no boat?"

"Ye could have walked from a village on the isle. Ye could have been brought here by whoever ye're working for," he returned, though her words momentarily gave him pause. Aye, she had an accent like he'd never heard before, but there were faraway lands he'd never ventured to. She was likely from one of those lands.

He jerked away from her unnerving touch and moved to the door. "I'll soon return. When I do, ye'll tell me the truth or I'll have ye sent tae the dungeons," he snapped, glowering at her before slamming the door behind him.

He stalked to his chamber, ushering out the chambermaid who was cleaning it and sinking down into a chair by the fireplace. He glared at the flames as if they could provide answers.

Who had sent her? The last conflict his clan had was with the northern clan of the isle, and they had amicably resolved it before the war with the Norse. As far as he knew, the clans of the surrounding isles were more concerned with the lingering threat of the Norse than with each other; it was the one positive thing that had emerged from the Norse-Scots conflict. Less infighting among the clans of the isles.

And he couldn't believe that Ulf distrusted him; there had been no suspicion in his eyes during his meeting. Ulf wouldn't betray Domhnall. *Nae the way ye're betraying him,* he thought darkly.

He pushed away the thought, rubbing his temples as he considered. Perhaps it was another Norseman who had sent her, trying to determine where his loyalties truly lie. But her odd accent didn't sound Norse.

Perhaps she's telling the truth.

A stiuireadh from another time? It sounded like a story his mother or nurse would tell him when he was a lad. He scowled, gritting his teeth. He would get her to tell him the truth; she couldn't hold on to such a fanciful tale for long.

Later that afternoon, Domhnall sat in the great hall with Ruarc, a clan noble and his most trusted advisor and friend. He'd not told him about Astrid, instead discussing the meeting he'd had with Ulf.

"And yer cousin believes that ye're on his side?" Ruarc asked.

"Aye."

"I ken 'tis difficult. I ken ye think ye're betraying yer blood," Ruarc said, giving him a look of sympathy. "But ye're doing what's right for yer people."

Domhnall said nothing. Ruarc was a close friend and knew him well, but he'd never know how difficult it was to betray your own blood. Ruarc was a Scot through and through. He had no Norse blood; he could trace his line back to the old Gaels. He didn't know what it was like to feel torn between two sides.

"Is there something else that ails ye?" Ruarc persisted, studying him closely.

Domhnall hesitated, debating whether to tell him about the lovely green-eyed prisoner he had in a guest chamber. But perhaps Ruarc would have insight.

"When I came back from meeting with my cousin, I found a lass on the shore," he said.

He proceeded to tell his cousin about Astrid's wild tale about being a stiuireadh from the future, and how he was determined to get the truth out of her.

When he was finished, he waited for Ruarc to agree with Domhnall's actions. Instead, Ruarc leaned back in his chair, looking pensive.

"I ken her story sounds strange," Ruarc said slowly. "But . . . I heard rumors when I was a lad. Rumors of people disappearing by the waters on the Isle of Skye. My nurse thought they were taken by the sidhe, but my mother would tell me that they were going tae another time. When I asked her how she kent, she told me she'd met one of them when

she was playing by the waters of Skye as a wee lass .
. . a man in strange clothing who spoke with a
strange tongue. She ran tae get her nurse, but when
she came back, he was gone. She told me she never
forgot about the man despite her nurse telling her it
was just a drunkard playing her for a fool."

He paused, holding Domhnall's gaze, allowing
his words to settle in. "I'm nae saying ye shouldnae
be suspicious," Ruarc continued, "but perhaps the
lass is telling the truth."

"How do I determine if she is?" Domhnall
asked, though he was still skeptical.

"'Tis simple," Ruarc said with a shrug. "Make
her prove that what she says is true."

CHAPTER 4

Astrid paced the length of the chamber, fear and anger battling for dominance of her emotions.

A large part of her didn't blame Domhnall for not believing her. If she wasn't a witch, she wouldn't believe any of her story herself. Yet another part of her was angry that he hadn't even *considered* that she might be telling the truth . . . something that caused her a surprising amount of hurt, which made no sense, given that she barely—didn't—even know him.

She stopped pacing, sinking down onto the bed and closing her eyes. She had considered using her backup plan of fleeing with the use of a spell when he'd threatened to throw her in the dungeons, but if she did that, she'd be right back where she started . . . back in her own time, plagued by visions of the past.

Astrid rubbed her fingers against her throbbing

temples, blinking back a sudden rush of tears. She'd gone years without practicing magic and could almost pretend she was normal. Why couldn't her magic just leave her be?

After the tragic events of her childhood, she'd managed to make a comfortable life for herself back in the twenty-first century. She'd moved from the small Northern California town, where her normal, non-magical Uncle Peter had raised her, to the bustling city of Los Angeles, where she'd gotten her medical degree and snagged a prized residency at a hospital there. At twenty-nine years old, she'd believed that she'd finally left her dark magical past behind her.

You'll get back to your life, she promised herself. She'd just have to do whatever it took to prove to Domhnall that she was telling the truth and get to the business of whatever time—her magic—wanted her to help him with.

The door abruptly flew open, and she stumbled to her feet in surprise, her heart leaping in her chest at the sight of Domhnall. A sudden burst of hope flared inside her. Maybe he believed her?

But his expression was thunderous as he entered, his brows knitted together in a scowl.

"The year," he practically spat, "is 1266."

Twelve sixty-six.

Astrid nearly sank to her knees. She'd ascertained that she was somewhere—some time—in the Middle Ages, but to hear confirmation that she was so far back in the past was still unfathomable.

Domhnall studied her for a long time as if searching for any trace of deceit in her expression. When she said nothing and just stood there, pale faced and trembling, he continued, "If what ye say is true, I want ye tae show me."

She blinked. "Show you?"

"Aye," he growled as he continued to step forward, his eyes filled with dark challenge. "If ye can perform magic as ye say, perform a spell. I want tae see it with my own eyes."

Astrid swallowed hard. It was a reasonable request. But other than coming back in time— through which she'd done nothing but jump into that fairy pool in Skye—her magic was still very raw. She'd only practiced a handful of spells before coming to this time, and each one had been difficult to cast.

She expelled a breath, thinking of the easiest spell she could cast. Looking around the room, her eyes landed on an unlit candle perched on a side table. She moved toward it as Domhnall kept his hawk-like gaze trained on her, crossing his arms over his broad chest.

Trying to ignore his distracting presence, she placed her hand above the candle and murmured the words of an Incendiary spell. "*Suidhich an aflame seo.*"

She waited for the telltale hum of electricity beneath her skin, but there was . . . nothing. Astrid repeated the spell. Still, nothing happened.

Panic coursed through her as her eyes locked

on Domhnall, who was now looking at her with smoldering fury. "I—I don't understand why it's not working," she whispered.

"Enough of the lies!" he roared. "Who are ye?"

"I told you!" she cried. "I'm a stiuireadh from the twenty-first century. I came here to—"

"Perhaps a night in the dungeons will help ye with the truth," he snapped.

He stepped forward, and her fear rose to a crescendo as he took her arm in a firm grip. She fought to release herself from his grip, her adrenaline spiking as she shot out a hand to ward him away from her.

It happened quickly. Domhnall's massive body lifted into the air, and an invisible force hurled him against the far wall.

A stunned silence filled the chamber and stretched. Astrid looked down at her hands and then up at Domhnall, who looked at her with pale-faced astonishment. How had she done that? She hadn't even thought of an Offensive spell. It was as if her magic had reacted out of an automatic protective instinct.

Propelled into action, she turned to the candle, murmuring the words of the Incendiary spell once more. This time candle roared to life with a strong flame. Heart hammering, she turned to the fireplace, where the flames were dying out, and issued another Incendiary spell. The flames obeyed her command immediately, roaring to life.

Only then did she turn to face Domhnall,

breathless, as his eyes went to the flames, and her, in astonishment.

"Now do you see," she said, "that I'm telling you the truth?"

Domhnall blinked, his face still white as he stumbled forward. He again studied the flames as if they could somehow provide answers. His hands shook as he lifted one to rake through his hair.

"I—I cannae deny what my eyes have just seen," he rasped, "but I need some time for what I've seen tae settle in my mind. I—I will see ye on the morrow."

"But—"

"I'll see ye on the morrow," he repeated firmly, still not looking at her. "Ye're no longer my prisoner, Astrid. But I ask ye nae tae leave."

He left her then, and Astrid watched him go, defeat settling onto her shoulders like a great weight. She thought she'd feel triumph after she convinced him of what she could do. Instead, she couldn't get the way he'd looked at her out of her mind. Like she was . . . unnatural. A freak.

That old insecurity, the hatred of what she was, came roaring back to the surface. She clenched her fists, closing her eyes. It was why she told no one what she was. It was why she wanted no part of witchcraft, time travel, any of it. She'd seen first-hand where it could all lead to.

Grief and anger filled her as she thought of her parents, emotions she quelled as she expelled a breath, blinking back tears. *You've convinced him.*

Now all you have to do is hope he lets you help him and then you can go back to your normal life.

~

THAT NIGHT, images of a dark figure who stalked her from the shadows dominated her dreams.

Despite the chill that hung in the chamber, she awoke bathed in a hot sweat. She took in her surroundings, closing her eyes. For a moment she'd hoped she'd wake up in her comfy Los Angeles condo. But no, she was in the thirteenth century, trying to convince a handsome Scot to allow her to help him with a mysterious, looming threat.

The same chambermaid who'd bathed her the day before entered, silently helping her dress in a high-waisted gown of deep green. The maid left her a tray filled with bread and hot broth before leaving her alone. It was odd having a personal maid, but Astrid was relieved that she hadn't tried to engage her in conversation, given her modern accent.

She'd just finished eating when the door swung open and Domhnall strode in, looking devastatingly handsome in his white tunic and dark breeches, his hair sexily tousled as if he'd been raking his hands through it. That searing awareness pierced her, and she had to willingly calm her racing heartbeat.

"As I told ye before, I cannae doubt what I've seen with my own eyes," he said, not looking at her.

"I thank ye for coming tae me, for trying tae help me. But my honor willnae allow me tae use unnatural means tae defeat my enemies, especially using magic—something I donnae understand nor can control myself. I'll have a guard escort ye safely tae wherever ye want tae go, but I do ask that ye leave and go back tae yer—tae this distant time ye say ye come from. I am laird and chieftain of my clan. I can handle what threatens it on my own, without the help of a—a witch."

CHAPTER 5

"There were more raids on several outer isles by the Norse last night," Ruarc said grimly.

Domhnall closed his eyes at Ruarc's words, expelling a heavy sigh. It was not long after he'd sent Astrid away; he now stood in the great hall with his men. Even though he told himself he was firm in his decision, he kept seeing the panicked look in her eyes when he'd told her to leave, how her lovely skin had paled. He'd turned his back on her and left after he'd issued his proclamation, expecting her to stop him with a plea. But she hadn't, and disappointment had pierced him at this, as if some part of him wanted her to convince him to allow her to stay.

'Tis for the best, he thought, forcing himself to concentrate on Ruarc's words and the other nobles, who had all stiffened at his words.

"I heard there's been an envoy sent to the Scottish king tae let him handle the matter," Seighlin, another of his nobles, said with a scowl. "This is becoming tae great of a matter for us tae handle on our own."

"Are ye a fool?" growled Duncan, another noble. "We cannae rely on the Scottish king. Aye, our isle falls under his protection by terms of the treaty, but the king has left this isle—and other surrounding isles—tae self-govern as we have for generations. The king may send a terse message tae the Norse, but that's all he'll do. The Scottish crown was bled dry by the war against the Norse. We have tae fight this as our fathers have done, and their fathers before them—on our own."

The other nobles uttered words of agreement until Domhnall held up his hand for silence.

"I understand yer concerns, Seighlin," Domhnall said, giving him a nod of understanding. "But what Duncan says is true—we have tae fight this threat on our own. We'll have tae join with other clans of the isles and work together tae fight off the men who donnae respect the treaty. And I have a spy working on my behalf tae keep me abreast of what the Norse are up tae."

He exchanged a look with Ruarc. His nobles didn't know that *he* was the spy. While he trusted his men with his life, it was too great of a risk for them to know of his subterfuge against his cousin.

Domhnall listened patiently as his nobles continued to voice their concerns—who could they trust to ally with, how to protect their lands, how to convince their men to fight when it became necessary—and did his best to reassure them.

They seemed reassured by each of his answers. They would have to rely on the honor of the clans of the isles. He would send more men to help them protect their lands. Fierce pride and protectiveness for the lands that had been theirs for generations would motivate their men to fight.

It was only when he'd made certain his nobles were firmly assured of his plan to defend their lands from the Norse that the meeting came to an end and his men filed out of the hall.

"Well?" Ruarc demanded as soon as they were alone. "Ye havenae said anything about the lass, Astrid. Was she being truthful with ye or is she in the dungeons?"

Domhnall scowled at Ruarc. A part of him had foolishly hoped that Ruarc wouldn't inquire about Astrid, that his focus would be entirely on the Norse threat.

"Did she demonstrate any magic?" Ruarc pressed.

"Aye," Domhnall said reluctantly.

Ruarc's eyes widened in amazement, and Domhnall recalled his own awe at what Astrid could do, an awe that hadn't left him. The sheer power she'd displayed by lifting his body from the ground . . .

"It . . . was like nothing I've ever seen," he confessed. "She hurled me across the room with her magic, set an unlit candle and a fire in the fireplace aflame. I cannae explain it."

"Where is she now?"

"I sent her away," Domhnall said, hoping that his regret at this didn't show through his tone.

"Why?" Ruarc demanded, looking at him with disbelief.

"I'll fight the Norse as my father did, and his father before him, without the use of such otherworldly things that I donnae understand—nor can control—such as magic. I've already sacrificed my honor tae betray my cousin."

Ruarc glared at him in silence for a few moments before he spoke, leaning forward. "Ye are the leader of this clan and my laird, but ye're also my friend, so I say this with respect. The Norsemen who ignore the treaty are the ones without honor. Do ye nae think they would use magical assistance if they could? Think of the lives that would be saved if—"

"I've made my decision," Domhnall growled. "Ye'll say no more of the matter. And ye'll keep what I've learned of Astrid tae yerself."

Ruarc returned his glare, getting to his feet. "Very well. But I think ye're being a fool."

Domhnall clenched his fists at his sides as Ruarc stalked out of the hall. As his oldest friend who was like a brother to him, Ruarc was the only man he'd allow to speak to him in such a manner.

Ruarc had been fostered at the castle as the eldest son of his father's closest friend. They were the same age and had grown up together; he was closer to Ruarc than he was to Ulf, though Ulf was blood. Ruarc was keen when it came to understanding men; he'd seen Ulf's greed long before Domhnall had, and that was why he was his closest advisor.

Perhaps he's right about Astrid as well, a phantom voice whispered in his mind, a whisper that he made himself ignore as he left the hall to attend to the matters of the day.

THAT EVENING, Domhnall sat at the head table in the great hall, trying to focus on the conversations around him. Despite his efforts not to, he'd thought of Astrid for the rest of the day, with Ruarc's words haunting him.

It wasn't only her magical ability that he thought of. He couldn't stop thinking about the beauty of her features and her startlingly green eyes, the tempting loveliness of her curves. He knew what he was feeling was more than regret; it was unquenched desire. He'd only been around her for a short time, but he wanted the lass as he'd wanted no other.

He forced his thoughts away from Astrid, taking in the men and women who were gathered in the hall for the evening feast. These were the men and women he was fighting for, who relied on him for leadership and protection. It was for these people that he was betraying his cousin, that he would defeat the Norse—with honor. Not magic.

He felt eyes on him and turned until his gaze locked on Moirna, a former mistress of his who stared at him with open longing. Moirna was the niece of one of his top nobles, Senan. He knew Senan had hoped he would wed the lass. But beyond a mild desire, he felt no great affection toward Moirna, something he would want to feel toward the lass who would become his wife.

Moirna smiled as their eyes locked. She was bonnie, aye, with lustrous chestnut-brown hair and sparkling dark eyes, but it was images of a green-eyed witch that filled his mind; how powerful she'd looked as she'd faced off with him, how desirable. He swallowed and took another large swig of his ale, averting his eyes. Perhaps he should bed Moirna again, just to get his mind off of Astrid. But the very thought sent an unsettling sensation through him, as if he'd just drank sour wine.

Surprised murmurings suddenly filled the hall, and Domhnall stiffened, following everyone's gazes to the entrance of the hall. Astonishment, disbelief, and a slight trace of relief, flooded him as his stunned gaze landed on Astrid.

She stood at the entrance of the great hall, looking sinful in a high-waisted ruby gown, her hair defiantly worn loose around her shoulders unlike the other women of the hall. Her green eyes locked with his, and unlike Moirna's look, it caused a firestorm of sensations to careen straight to his groin.

Ignoring the stares directed her way, she made her way over to him. A guard who hovered behind him stepped forward, but he waved him away as Astrid reached his table.

"My laird," she said, her voice bold, though he saw traces of uncertainty lurking in the depths of her eyes. "I've decided that I'll stay."

CHAPTER 6

$\mathcal{A}$strid looked down at Domhnall, hoping she displayed more confidence than she felt. Her hands shook and her breathing was unsteady, but she evenly held Domhnall's blue gaze.

She had almost left after he'd sent her away, her frustration was so great. The memory of that dark dream she'd had of that mysterious, shadowy figure, and the certainty that *something* evil was coming stopped her. She also knew that once she returned to her own time, visions and nightmares of the past would once again assail her. She would know no peace until she obeyed what her magic and time wanted her to do—stay put and help the stubborn, gorgeous Scot.

And there was also the undeniable pull she felt toward Domhnall, that sense of both familiarity and desire.

When Domhnall's guard had come to fetch

her, she'd lied and informed him she wasn't feeling well, and the laird wanted her to stay longer until she was feeling better. She'd thought the guard would immediately tell Domhnall and half expected him to show up in her chamber, furiously demanding that she leave. But he hadn't, meaning the guard must have taken her at her word, buying her much-needed time.

She'd spent the entire day tucked away in her chamber trying to figure out how to get Domhnall to accept her help, until she'd come up with a solution that might work. She'd decided it was best to approach him at that evening's feast in the great hall; he'd be less likely to dismiss her in front of his people.

Now he looked at her with a mixture of disbelief, annoyance, and dare she hope—pride? She could have sworn she saw his lips slightly curve into a hint of a smile before they turned into a scowl.

After a long moment, he turned to a broad-shouldered, red-haired man at his side, who studied her with open curiosity and, interestingly, admiration.

"Ruarc, let the lass have yer seat," Domhnall said.

Relief flowed through her as the man, Ruarc, got to his feet and moved to another chair, allowing her to sit down next to Domhnall.

"Smile," Domhnall said in a low voice, "so that

everyone thinks ye're just a guest I've invited, and they stop staring at ye."

Astrid forced a smile, and soon the other guests in the hall went back to their own conversations, though some stares lingered.

"I know you wanted me to leave. But please, consider keeping me here for a fortnight," Astrid said, keeping her voice low enough for only him to hear. "You don't have to use my abilities if you don't want. In my time, I'm a doctor—a healer. I can help with any sick people you have here in the castle or in the nearby village. You can use that as an excuse as to why I'm here."

Doctors were a valuable commodity in any time, but especially in the infectious and disease-ridden medieval period. She knew her medical knowledge would go a long way here, and it was something she felt comfortable with. As for her magic, she hoped that this threat she sensed was coming would force Domhnall's hand in accepting her help before the fortnight was up.

"Like a midwife? I already have—"

"No, more than that," she interrupted. "I can help with childbirth if needed, but I'm a general practitioner—that means I can help with all sorts of ailments. Do you have a healer who lives here in the castle?"

Domhnall's skeptical look lingered, and her frustration spiked. She knew female doctors who weren't midwives were practically unheard of in this time, and the notion of socially accepted female doctors was still centuries away.

"There's a healer in the village who I call upon whenever I need him," he said finally.

"Well, you can call upon me. And instead of having to wait on a messenger, I'll be right here in the castle."

"And ye willnae try tae persuade me tae use yer —abilities?"

"No," she lied, holding his gaze. "Only if you ask me."

"I willnae," he said, though she noticed he looked away as he spoke the words. "Verrae well. Ye can stay a fortnight, and then ye'll go on yer way."

"Agreed."

Domhnall looked satisfied, and Astrid had to push away the surprising amount of hurt she felt at his determination to send her away.

He gestured to a servant, who approached and set down a plate of roasted vegetables and fish before her. She studied it nervously; she'd only had bowls of broth and stew in this time. What would an actual meal be like?

"The food isnae poison, lass," Domhnall said, giving her a look of wry amusement.

Astrid flushed and took a bite of fish, which tasted like salted herring. It was delicious, surprisingly so. She continued to eat, not realizing how hungry she'd been.

"Ye're quite brave," Domhnall said, taking a

swig of his ale, eyeing her as she ate, "tae have defied me and remained here."

"I can be just as stubborn as you," she returned, and his mouth quirked in another hint of a smile.

Her gaze strayed to the various guests in the hall, many of whom were still casting curious glances her way. "Who are your guests?"

"Clan nobles and their families," Domhnall said, pride shining in his eyes as he took them in. "All loyal tae this clan for generations, going back tae the time of Somerled."

Astrid bit her lip, resisting the urge to tell him that she could help protect them if he allowed her to use her magic. Instead, she kept silent and tried not to stare too much, to concentrate on her food, but it still felt surreal to be centuries in the past, to move among the people who lived here, hundreds of years before she was born. She watched as they conversed, joked, and laughed among themselves. What was it like to live in this time?

Her gaze slid to Domhnall, who was now engaged in conversation with Ruarc. What was it like to be a laird and chieftain, which in this time had to be the equivalent of serving as a mayor or a governor?

Domhnall stopped talking to Ruarc and gave her a slight scowl at her stare; she forced herself to look away. She couldn't blame him for his obvious irritation with her. He had a load of responsibility on his shoulders, and Astrid must have turned his world upside down. *You have no choice,* she reminded herself, as doubt once again seized her. *Your magic wants you to stay and assist him— whether he wants you to or not.*

The meal soon came to an end, with many of the guests coming to bid farewell to Domhnall before they left, their gazes lingering on her with curiosity. One attractive woman in particular gave her a blistering glare, and she wondered, with a stab of something that felt like jealousy, if this woman was Domhnall's mistress.

But she didn't have too much time to ponder this as Domhnall gestured for her to follow as he rose from his seat. He said nothing as he accompanied her from the great hall to her chamber, where he gave her a hard look.

"I meant what I said in the great hall," he said firmly. "Ye're here for a fortnight and no more."

"Yes, you made yourself very clear," she said, another stab of hurt piercing her.

Domhnall started to walk away, but she couldn't stop herself, reaching out to grab his arm. Electricity raced through her veins at the feel of his muscular arm, and she quickly withdrew her hand.

"Is it truly honor that makes you not want to use my magic—or fear?" she asked.

Domhnall's eyes narrowed, and he took a step forward, causing a heated awareness to spiral throughout her body. "I donnae understand what ye can do, aye, but I donnae fear it. Fear has no place in the heart of a chieftain; my father taught me that. I donnae ken how it is in this time ye purport tae be from, but in this time, honor is everything. And I willnae sacrifice my honor, no more than I already have."

More than he already had? Before she could question what he meant by that, he turned on his heel and stalked away.

Astrid watched him go, wariness settling over her. She had her work cut out for her, and not just to get Domhnall to trust her enough to use her abilities . . . but to stem her overwhelming pull of desire toward the stubborn man.

After their heated encounter, Astrid assumed Domhnall would allow the fortnight to pass without calling on her services out of spite, but to her surprise he sent for her the very next morning. As she approached his chamber, she silently prayed that he'd changed his mind and would use her magical ability.

When she entered the chamber, which appeared to be a study of some sort, he was standing by the window not looking at her as he studied a parchment in his hands.

"My advisor Ruarc needs a healer tae tend tae his pregnant wife Siomha. She's been ill as of late and her midwife cannae help; she's away for the birth of one of my nobles' sons. Ye can help her, aye?"

A mix of disappointment and relief filled her.

Disappointment at his not using her magic, and relief that her medical services were needed. Magic was still new to her, but medicine was her passion, and something she could do well.

"Yes," she said.

Still not looking at her, which caused her more hurt than it should have, he dismissed her, and a male servant accompanied her to another chamber at the far end of the castle, which Astrid realized was larger than she'd initially estimated.

A young chambermaid ushered her inside.

The same man who had been at Domhnall's side last night, Ruarc, stood there, hovering at the bedside of a young blonde woman who looked close to six months pregnant. The woman, who she guessed was Siomha, gave Astrid a look of such . . . *knowing* that it was disconcerting.

"I'll leave ye," Ruarc said, leaning down to place a loving kiss on his wife's head. He moved past Astrid, giving her a polite nod.

Astrid approached Siomha, taking a seat by her side and giving the woman a kind smile, which she returned. "How far along are—" Astrid began, but Siomha interrupted her.

"Ye're a stiuireadh," she said calmly.

Astrid stiffened with surprise. She'd thought Domhnall wouldn't have told a soul about her, but he clearly had. A current of fear rippled through her. If enough people knew what she was . . .

"Oh, ye have nothing tae fear," Siomha assured her, seeming to read her mind as she gave her another smile. "Ruarc would never betray Domhnall's trust—he didnae tell me. I sensed yer presence."

"Sensed?" Astrid echoed, baffled.

"Aye. My ancestors were stiuireadh, direct from the line of druids. I donnae have any magic of my own, but I have echoes of the Sight . . . I can sometimes see things that are tae come. Something dark is coming tae the isles, something that threatens us all. Ye're the one that can stop it."

Astrid paced the length of her chamber, arms wrapped tightly around herself. She closed her eyes, shaking.

I can't do this, she thought frantically. *I just want to go home.*

Siomha's revelation had been a bombshell.

"Ye're here tae bring peace tae the isles, tae stop the Norse. But ye willnae do it alone. I cannae see it clearly, but ye are the one who will bring about an alliance between the witches and the lairds of the isles. I've seen visions of it," Siomha told her.

Astrid had frozen as the full implication of her words settled in. Unable to come up with a coherent response, she'd excused herself and stumbled out of Siomha's chamber.

Now, her heart pounded with the fury of a sledgehammer against her ribcage. She knew exactly what Siomha was referring to.

She should have realized. As soon as Domhnall

had told her what year it was, she should have known.

Astrid closed her eyes, mentally crawling through her childhood memories, to memories she had long since banished.

"There was a Pact made centuries ago, between the stiuireadh and the lairds of the Scottish Isles, to help ward off the Norse invaders," a witch in her coven had told her and several other children as they sat around her, listening to tales of past stiuireadh.

Domhnall had told her the present year was 1266, and by the weather she'd gleaned it was early fall. That meant it was not long after the Norse and Scots signed a peace treaty. Based on what she knew of this time and the circumstances surrounding the Pact, the Norse were still a threat even after the treaty was signed. Since the Pact clearly hadn't happened yet . . . *Astrid* must be the one who had to put it into motion.

She pressed a hand to her mouth, shutting her eyes.

How could she, a weak and nonpracticing stiuireadh, who'd only come to this time to stop visions and nightmares from assailing her, be so influential in such an important magical and historic event?

There has to be some mistake. Siomha must have meant someone else. I can't be responsible for something so monumental.

But her gut instinct, the same instinct that

made her feel a powerful connection to Domhnall, the same instinct that had brought her here, told her that this had to be the case. She thought of all the images she'd seen in her visions of the past—the approaching ships, the battles on land and at sea. Time, fate, and magic had guided her to this time and place for a reason.

She was meant to set the Pact into motion.

Overwhelmed, Astrid swayed on her feet as blackness descended on her like an ominous cloud. She wasn't sure how much time had passed when she heard a panicked voice—Domhnall's voice.

"Astrid? Astrid!"

His voice brought a sense of calm with it, and the darkness gradually cleared.

Astrid opened her eyes to find herself in Domhnall's arms. She was on the floor of her chamber, and Domhnall held her, his blue eyes filled with concern.

"Are ye unwell?"

She looked at him, trying to steady her still rapid breathing.

It's up to me to stop another potential war. But I can't do it, she wanted to scream. *I'm not the one who should be helping you. I don't have the power or the knowledge.*

But she said none of this.

"I need to tell you something," she whispered. "Something about the future."

❀

DOMHNALL, Ruarc, and Siomha sat in silence as Astrid stood before them in Domhnall's private chamber.

Domhnall had asked her to repeat her story, in its entirety, several times. Siomha was looking at her with a look of abject calm as she already knew what Astrid had told them, while both Ruarc and Domhnall were pale.

Astrid had just told them of a future in which the Norse were successfully defeated with the help of the stiuireadh, ushering in a Pact that would forever bind the lairds of the isles and the stiuireadh.

"She speaks the truth," Siomha said as the silence stretched. "I've seen it in my dreams."

Domhnall stiffened in surprise, looking back and forth between Siomha and Ruarc. Ruarc gave Domhnall an apologetic smile.

"I've kent of Siomha's ability of the Sight, but she wanted to keep it between us. 'Tis why I believed in Astrid's abilities when ye told me of them."

"It's best if nae many ken of what I can do," Siomha added, giving him an apologetic look of her own.

Domhnall still looked quietly stunned, but gave Ruarc and Siomha nods of understanding.

Astrid waited, tense; he was the one she needed to believe her. And as he met her eyes, she could see that he did.

He closed his eyes, rubbing his temples before

he spoke. "My line is both Norse and Gael—my father's side Gael, my mother's Norse. My Norse cousin and his allies want tae take back lands given tae the Scottish king in the recent treaty. I'm pretending tae go along with my cousin, but in truth I'm working against him."

"The treaty only increased resentment among the Norse," Ruarc added. "While formal colonization stopped, there have still been raids. And the raids have begun tae increase."

"But according tae what ye say, we win the war," Domhnall said, studying her.

"Not so fast," she said, holding up her hand. "Time isn't a straight line—it can twist and change. If we fail, the future may turn out very different. It's not set in stone. Some things can't be changed, others can. There are witches called fiosaiche—seers, who monitor events in time and can tell what can and cannot be changed. Siomha has traces of this ability. I'm not a fiosaiche, but I can only assume that since my magic wants me here, this is an event that can be altered, for better or worse."

She allowed her words to settle for several moments before continuing. "Now that you've heard me out, are you willing to use my abilities? The abilities of other stiuireadh I find?"

Domhnall looked conflicted, his brows knitted together in a frown, his face still pale.

"Magic is as natural as breathing, my laird," Siomha spoke up, her tone gentle. "The verrae fact that it exists makes it natural. Astrid was sent here for a reason."

Astrid gave Siomha a smile, liking her even more. Ruarc reached for Siomha's hand, lifting it to his lips in a kiss.

"And I believe Siomha. I've told ye, it would be foolish tae nae use what we can tae bring about peace," he said.

Domhnall stood, pacing briefly before stopping in front of her. "I confess I still feel unease at the thought of using abilities I donnae understand, abilities I donnae think are natural, but as chieftain and laird, 'tis my duty tae bring about peace. Tae bring about this future in which the people of the isles can live in peace. How do we make this future come about?"

Relief and anxiety swept over Astrid. This was what she wanted, Domhnall's cooperation, but the sheer magnitude of what she had to do still overwhelmed her. She made herself push past her fear as she addressed them.

"You need to keep working together with other lairds and clans who have been attacked—alliances are key. And I think you should keep the subterfuge up with your cousin. Any knowledge from him will be valuable."

Domhnall nodded his agreement. "And what do ye need?"

"I need to find other stiuireadh in this time. Since the Pact happened, I know they're here. I just need to find them."

"I can help ye," Siomha said. "I ken of one who resides on this isle."

Both Domhnall and Ruarc looked at her with surprise. Siomha just gave them a serene smile.

"There are more of us with magic than ye ken," she said simply.

"That would be wonderful," Astrid said, smiling. "Thank you.

Ruarc and Siomha left them alone, and Domhnall moved over to the window, his troubled gaze finding hers after a long stretch of silence.

"Ye think it is wise what I am doing, betraying my cousin?"

"You're not betraying him," Astrid said with a frown. "He's the one who's being dishonorable, violating the terms of the treaty. By being a double agent, you're protecting your people."

He frowned. "Double agent?"

"It's a term from the future," she said. "It means exactly what you're doing—using subterfuge to make the enemy believe you're working with him."

"'Tis odd tae think of my cousin as an enemy," Domhnall said with a sigh. He raked a hand through his hair as his gaze shifted to her, his troubled look shifting to one of curiosity. "How is it? This future of yers? Ye said ye were a healer?"

"Yes," she said, a pang of longing piercing her. "I had just completed my studies, and I was on my way to becoming a GP—a doctor."

"Ye have a family in this future? A husband?"

he asked, something dark flaring in his eyes before it was gone again.

"No. My uncle raised me, but he died a couple of years ago, and I don't have any close family left. Still, I like my life there. It's a normal life . . . despite what I am. And I want a normal life after—" Flashes of memory from her childhood pierced her thoughts, and she had to forcibly push them away. "It's a life I want to get back to. My magic . . . it *assailed* me to come here. Imagine an invisible force, like a gale of wind, pushing you in a direction you don't want to go. And if you don't obey it, it just keeps pushing."

Frustration surged within her, and she blinked back tears. Domhnall strode across the room until he was only inches away from her, giving her a look of sympathy.

"I'm . . . sorry," he said quietly. "It must be hard for ye, lass. I ken I wasnae kind tae ye before. It was just difficult for me tae believe—"

"No. I understand. I'm a time-traveling witch, and even I don't believe it sometimes," she said, forcing a smile.

"I ken ye were forced tae be here by yer— magic. And I thank ye. I hope that we can end this and bring peace tae the isles. And then ye can get back tae the time ye belong."

He smiled down at her, making her heart perform a catapult in her chest. Her breath hitched in her throat as his eyes dipped to her mouth. The moment seemed to become frozen in time, and then everything was set into motion again as he leaned forward to capture her lips with his.

His kiss was fervent and demanding, and Astrid's pulse thrummed wildly as she responded, her arms seeming to have a life of their own as they wound around his neck.

His arms went to her waist, pressing her flush against his muscular body, and the fiery heat of arousal coursed through her, seizing her very core. He tasted like ale and honey, and she couldn't get enough of the feel of him; his firm lips on hers, his tongue exploring her mouth, the broadness of his chest pressed against her. It seemed as if time, that pesky force of nature that held her prisoner, had completely frozen, and there was only this moment.

When he released her, she could barely breathe, and her heartbeat was a furious drumbeat in her ears. His blue eyes were alight with desire as they roamed over her face, and he leaned forward as if to kiss her again, when there was a knock on the door and the inquiring voice of his servant.

The knock caused the heated moment to dissipate, and Astrid forced herself to step back.

"I—I should go," she said hastily, and before he could reply, she hurried out of his chamber, her entire body still pulsing with desire.

CHAPTER 8

*D*omhnall watched Astrid leave his chamber, the need for her still coursing throughout his body. He ached for more than her sweet mouth . . . he wanted to bed the beautiful witch. For several tantalizing moments he allowed himself to imagine taking her to his bed, kissing her breathless, and tasting the sweetness between her thighs before claiming her body with his own.

He had to force the images out of his head as his cock stirred with arousal. There was much to be done, and he didn't have time to lust after Astrid. He should have restrained himself and not allowed himself to kiss her. Because now that he'd had a taste . . .

Gritting his teeth with frustration, he stalked to his door to answer it, ordering the hovering servant to send for his messenger.

"I need ye tae send these messages post haste,"

he told Aodh, the man who served as his most trusted messenger when he arrived later, handing him several carefully rolled pieces of parchment. He'd composed messages to the other chieftain and laird of Barra Isle, Neacal, and another one to Ulf. "Keep them safe."

"Aye, my laird," Aodh said, with a respectful bow of his head.

Domhnall watched him leave, anxiety tightening his belly. With Neacal working alongside him, he hoped to organize a strategic alliance to protect all of Barra.

Neacal's clan, Clan Laidirh, had once been the mortal enemy of his clan, fighting for generations over the scant but fertile lands of Barra. But ever since the conflict with the Norse, they'd formed an alliance. Ruarc's wife Siomha was a cousin of Neacal's; it was another thing that linked the two clans.

He wouldn't tell Neacal about the stiuireadh, not yet; he suspected that Astrid would know when it was best to inform the other chieftains of their existence.

A pull of something that was more than desire swept over him as he thought of the newfound trust he had in Astrid. Only days ago he'd been ready to imprison her for her seeming lies, something that made him feel a stab of guilt now.

He'd lied to her about not having fear of her magic; indeed, he did fear it. When magic was spoken of by those who believed in it, it was always with fear and association with darkness and evil. There was nothing dark or evil about Astrid; he may have only known her briefly, but he could tell she was all kindness and light.

And beauty, he thought, his cock stirring once more as he thought of their kiss and what he wanted to do to that desirable body of hers.

He forced aside the distracting thoughts, recalling that according to Astrid, magic would become an intrinsic part of the isles when it came to bringing peace. Peace. Something he ached for after the long conflict with the Norse. Something his people deserved, that all the people who dwelled on the isles deserved.

And he would do what he must to bring it about.

"I'll be meeting with Neacal in three days' time. I want our clans tae unite tae fight this renewed threat from the Norse," Domhnall informed his nobles.

It was midday the next day; Aodh had returned quickly with a response from Neacal. After discussing the message with Ruarc, he'd called for a meeting with his top nobles.

His nobles looked pleased at his announcement. Domhnall met Ruarc's gaze, ignoring the guilt that pierced him at the information he'd withheld, that he was using the aid and advice of a stiuireadh. He'd decided it was best to tell the nobles the non-magical part of their renewed offense against the Norse for now, and Ruarc had agreed.

After he answered some questions from his nobles about the meeting with Neacal and they'd discussed clan matters, his men dispersed.

Domhnall stiffened with surprise as Astrid entered the hall, moving past his men who gave her curious—and appreciative—looks as she approached Domhnall.

She looked breathtaking in a high-waisted heather-gray gown, her long dark curls now plaited into a long braid down her back. The dress did nothing but highlight those tempting curves of hers, and he had to ignore the lust that swept over him, filling him with instant arousal.

"Are you meeting with the other chieftain of Barra?" she asked without preamble, giving him an accusatory look.

He forced himself to lift his gaze from her bosom to her angered gaze, narrowing his eyes. "Were ye listening at the door, lass?"

"Yes," she said, without a flicker of shame. "I went looking for you, and your manservant told me you were here. I was waiting until you were done and I overheard your discussion. Domhnall, I need to be informed of these things." She hesitated for a moment, lowering her eyes as she continued. "Just because we—we shared a kiss, doesn't mean I'm here for anything else than to help."

"I ken that," he returned, ignoring the surprising shard of hurt that pierced him at her words. "I didnae want tae tell my nobles about the stiuireadh yet. I donnae ken how they will take it. Remember, I didnae believe ye when ye first arrived. I need them in accord with the non-magical part of the defense plan before I tell them more."

"Fine. But I should at least come with you when you meet with this chieftain."

Domhnall glowered at her. He was chieftain; not even Ruarc challenged his authority on such matters.

She has magical abilities, abilities ye need, that can help with this fight, he reminded himself, taking a breath to calm himself.

"I'll inform ye of what happens. It would look odd, and suspicious, tae take an unkent lass tae such a meeting," he said shortly. He started to move past her, to not only end the discussion but to get out of her distracting presence. But she reached out to place a hand on his arm, sending a rush of heat through his body.

"As a stiuireadh, there are things I can . . . sense about people. It's plagued me all my life even when I wasn't practicing magic. Now I can put that skill to use. It's best if I'm there, so I can hear everything that's said. Tell them I'm a healer tending to one of your men recently wounded. But I'm coming with you, Domhnall. I didn't travel all this time to sit in my chamber."

He scowled at her, and she returned it. Neacal was an honorable man and posed no threat, but he was still wary. He was protective when it came to Astrid even though she possessed magical strengths he himself wasn't capable of.

The silence stretched as Astrid held his gaze, defiance shining in her lovely eyes.

"Verrae well, lass," he said grudgingly. "But ye'll linger behind me and my men and nae say a word, aye?"

She nodded her agreement. The defiance left her eyes, but instead of relief there was . . . vulnerability. A hint of fear.

"Astrid?"

"I'm just overwhelmed," she confessed. "I feel as if so much is dependent on my ability to help you. But I'm still magically weak, and I don't know the ins and outs of this time. I don't like that lives depend on whether I succeed or fail." She closed her eyes briefly, rubbing her temples before giving him a weary smile. "I shouldn't have told you that, should I? Not when I just convinced you to let me come with you."

"I'd be afeared if ye didnae have doubts," he said, returning her smile. And though he'd tried to leave just a moment ago, he found himself extending his hand. "Come. I ken of a place that will ease yer fears."

She took his hand, and warmth enveloped him, a warmth that felt like the soothing fire that roared from the hearth in his chamber.

He kept her hand in his as he led her out of the hall and the castle, taking her through the courtyard. He had a guard lift the rear gates for them, and he led her to a section of rocky shore that surrounded the castle, where he reluctantly released her hand.

The blue waters that surrounded the castle sparkled beneath the bright sunlight, a vast sky dotted by patches of clouds stretched over the islets and islands in the near distance. The air smelled of salt, and there was only the sound of the waves lapping against the rocky shore, the distant call of birds.

He came here when he needed time alone to reflect; he'd come here after the death of his father, and after he'd made the fateful decision to work against Ulf.

He stood back, watching as Astrid stepped forward, taking in the surroundings with awe.

"This is beautiful," she said, shaking her head with amazement.

As are ye, he thought, admiring the way a few stray strands of her curls danced around her face in the breeze. He allowed himself to take in her beauty for another long moment before speaking.

"Aye," he agreed, pride swelling over him. "Farraige Castle was built generations ago by my ancestor, Diarmadh. It began as a temporary fortification against his enemies before becoming his home."

"You grew up here?"

"Aye. 'Tis always been my home. Ruarc, my

cousin and I would swim in these waters when we were lads despite the nurse and my mother telling us how dangerous it was, how we'd be pulled under if the waters were tae take us. But my bloodline is of the sea. I ken it well; I respect it enough tae ken when 'tis dangerous."

"Young men are the same in any era," Astrid said with a chuckle. "Proud and reckless."

"Tell me more about this time ye're from," he said, curiosity tugging at him.

"What exactly do you want to know about it?"

"Where do people live? Do the wealthy have manor homes and castles and the poor live in cottages?"

"Not much has changed in that regard," she said with a smile. "Most people live in regular-sized homes or apartments. The very rich live in large homes—mansions. Most people don't live in castles in my time, not even the rich. They're more like a relic of another time. People visit them—like museums."

"Museums?"

"Places where people view things from the past."

"That seems like an odd thing tae do," Domhnall said, frowning.

"People have an appreciation for the past in my time. Things are . . . easier, so there's time to do things like visit the museums. For many people, at least people in my country, there's an abundance of food. Technology has also made things run smoother."

He didn't understand most of what she'd said, but a pang pierced him at the longing in her eyes. This was clearly a time she missed, a time she wanted to return to.

"Ye must be looking forward tae returning."

"Yes," she said, though her voice sounded strained as she added, "it's my home."

Ignoring the lingering sting he felt at her words, he listened intently as she continued to describe this distant time; the types of people who would live and how they would live, the different places that would come to be, many of which weren't yet discovered.

At his prodding, she told him more about how she'd traveled through time, by leaping into one of the fairy pools of Skye, which was called a "portal" that transported people through time. He'd long heard rumors of mystical occurrences around the fairy pools. Before he met Astrid, he'd assumed they were just rumors; he now knew better.

Astrid described time travel as a rushing darkness, and then the feeling of plummeting through air as if falling from a great height.

Though awe filled him at her words, he was mostly enthralled by just the soft timbre of her voice, and watching her. He could watch her for an eternity; those sensual lips, the intense green of her eyes, the enticing curves of her body.

"Now it's your turn. Tell me more about this

time," she said, forcing him to quell his lustful thoughts.

"I can only tell ye of my lands, my people," he said, feeling a slight ripple of shame. She had traveled through time; he had rarely ventured off his lands.

But Astrid only looked intrigued, leaning forward. "Tell me," she said, looking at him with such eagerness that he couldn't help but smile.

"The clan is of the utmost importance; the people of the isle ken they are protected, and 'tis my honor tae protect them. Honor is valued above all; 'tis why 'tis so difficult for me tae betray my cousin, though I ken it must be done."

Astrid listened intently as he continued, telling her of his ancestors who had built this castle and claimed the lands for their own, soon becoming a Norse-Gaelic culture that was independent of even Scotland. That was changing, especially since the war and the aid of the Scottish king to ward off the Norse; it was the frequent incursions of the Norse that was forcing his people more to Scotland's side.

He didn't realize how much time had passed until the sun began to sink beyond the horizon. He realized he was reluctant to leave her side; Astrid's presence made him forget the stressors of his duties, the responsibility that had become a great weight to bear.

But he made himself accompany her back to her chamber, resisting the urge to kiss her as he bade her a good night.

As he turned and walked away from her chamber, his heart grew heavy as he reminded himself that her time here was temporary, and as much as he ached for her, he must continue to keep quelling his growing need for the bonnie witch.

"**W**hat is it ye want?"

Astrid stared down at the petite, freckled, red-haired woman who glared up at her. She barely came up to Astrid's shoulders, and would have been adorable if it weren't for the hostile look she was giving Astrid.

Astrid swallowed hard, turning back to glance at the distant lone figure of Ruarc. He'd accompanied her here to meet with Fyfa, the local stiuireadh Siomha had referred her to, not wanting the pregnant Siomha to leave the castle. They'd decided that until the nobles knew of the stiuireadh, Domhnall shouldn't accompany her to see Fyfa to avoid scrutiny.

A part of her was relieved that Domhnall wasn't with her, another part disappointed. The sexual tension between them had only grown since their kiss, a kiss she'd thought about nonstop.

Never had she experienced a pull of heated

yearning like the one she'd felt when she was in his arms. Just the memory of his mouth against hers caused a tingle between her thighs. During their long conversation the day before, she'd had to fight to keep her eyes off of his mouth, to quell the steady hum of desire that coursed through her veins at his nearness.

Now Astrid forced her thoughts away from Domhnall and turned back to Fyfa, who was glowering at her. Siomha had assured them that Fyfa knew she was coming, but Fyfa was looking at Astrid as if she were an enemy combatant encroaching upon her territory.

"Siomha sent you a message telling you I was coming," Astrid said, trying to ignore her blatant hostility, giving her the friendliest smile she could manage. "I'm—"

"I ken who ye are," Fyfa practically growled. "I like Siomha, 'tis why I agreed tae see ye. But I want no part of helping ye." She took a menacing step forward, her eyes narrowing. "My line is of the fiosaiche—seers. I kent ye were coming. And I ken of the darkness in ye."

Horror bloomed in Astrid's chest; she took a faltering step back.

"I see that ye ken of what I speak. I'll nae help someone like ye. Get out of this time and go back tae where ye're from, and take yer evil with ye."

Fyfa shut the door. Astrid just stared at it, panic and dread clawing its way through her chest. She closed her eyes, pressing shaking fingers to her forehead. She should have known that someone would figure out who she was . . . *what* she was.

"Astrid?"

Ruarc's voice was heavy with concern as she approached him a moment later, keeping her gaze averted so he wouldn't see the torment in her eyes.

"What did she say?"

Astrid tried to form words, but what could she say? *She knows there is evil in me. She knows the true reason I've avoided magic my entire life. She knows everything that I hate about myself.*

"She's unable to help," Astrid said finally, still not looking at him as he helped her up onto her horse. "It's all right. I'll keep searching."

She was thankful he didn't press or attempt to talk to her during the brief ride back to the castle, though he did give her a long, probing look as he helped her down from her horse in the castle's courtyard.

Avoiding his gaze, Astrid hurried out of the courtyard to her chamber, where she sank down onto the floor, wrapping her arms around her body as she rocked herself back and forth.

You're not them, Astrid, her Uncle Peter would whisper to her, rocking her back and forth in his arms whenever she awoke from nightmares as a child. *You're not your parents.*

But now, as she recalled the hatred in Fyfa's eyes, she couldn't help but feel as if her parents' crimes were her own.

Memories that she'd tried for so long to

suppress rose to the surface, like drowning swim-mers coming to the surface for much-needed air.

The screams of the man her father killed before her eyes. His pleas for mercy. Her parents linking hands as they recited a spell over his tortured body. The madness in their eyes as they turned toward her, stretching out their hands, urging her to join them. Her terror as she ran, desperate to get as far away from them as she could.

Astrid stumbled to her feet, feeling the rise of a panic attack. She needed air.

She stumbled out of her chamber, making her way to the section of rocky shore that Domhnall had taken her to the day before. She found a place to sit, trying to calm her panicked, racing thoughts. But she kept hearing the man's screams, seeing her parents' looks of dark glee in her mind's eye.

She didn't know how long she was sitting there before she felt a presence behind her; she knew without looking up that it was Domhnall. He sat down at her side, but somehow seemed to sense that she needed silence, for which she was grateful.

After an interminable stretch of silence, Astrid spoke, her voice barely above a whisper, the words spilling from her lips like water.

"My parents were *aingidh* . . . what the stiuireadh call dark witches. It's why Fyfa turned me away; she believes I have the same darkness in me. When you have the power of time travel and magic . . . it's very easy to corrupt you. That's one reason there are covens, to contain such power. My parents were obsessed with the power they had to travel through time. They wanted to go back and change events in the past to acquire wealth for themselves in the present, which is forbidden among the stiuireadh, especially when you try to change things that can't or shouldn't be undone. They were expelled from our local coven, and that's when they grew more dangerous. One night . . ."

Astrid closed her eyes and took a deep, shuddering breath before forcing herself to continue.

" . . . there was a man. He was a member of our coven, and he was threatening to tell the coven leaders that my parents were still using dark magic. They—they tortured him before killing him with their magic. I ran away that night, went to the local coven leader and told her everything. Killing another witch is the most severe crime you can commit as a stiuireadh. I pleaded for their lives despite what they did, so the coven leader exiled them to a distant time from which they couldn't return—and one they likely wouldn't survive. They never told me what time period that was, but I was told they died there."

Grief and guilt momentarily enveloped her, and she clenched her fists at her sides as tears threatened to spill. "My uncle took me in, raised me, showed me what love was, what normalcy was. But I never forgot. What they did haunted my nightmares, and I feared I would turn out like them. So I turned my back on magic, time travel, all of it. I became a doctor, thinking I could somehow make up for what they did by healing people."

Domhnall said nothing, and dread tightened her belly. Would he send her away? But the hand she felt on her chin was gentle as he tilted her head up to meet his gaze.

"Listen tae me, lass. I may nae ken nothing of magic or time travel, but I do ken that we're nae our parents. We make our own path in life. And I ken that just by coming tae this time, whether yer magic compelled ye tae or nae, means ye're a good person. I'm sorry for nae trusting ye before. But ye cannae let yer parents' darkness hold ye prisoner."

His words were similar to what her uncle had told her countless times, words she had tried to tell herself, but hearing it from Domhnall gave her an even greater sense of comfort.

"Thank you," she whispered.

He reached out to pull her into the warm circle of his arms, and they just sat for several long moments. Along with the desire that pulsed through her at his nearness, a calm settled over Astrid. And though she still felt tormented over what her parents had done in the past, Domhnall's words had given her a momentary peace.

"I'm going to try again with Fyfa," she said finally, pulling out of his arms, though her body ached to lean closer.

She had no choice but to approach Fyfa again. If future events were to unfold the way they were supposed to, she needed the help of other witches. And she had the feeling that Fyfa knew of others.

"Good," he said. "Get some rest. I'll see ye on the morrow. And Astrid," he added, his gaze lingering on her face, "remember what I said. Ye are nae yer parents—nor their sins."

"I'll try," she murmured.

Domhnall gave her a smile that she returned. As their eyes locked, something seemed to shift in the air between them. Her pulse fluttered as his eyes darkened with lust, her mouth going dry with want as Domhnall leaned forward, claiming her mouth with his.

Astrid clung to him, her heart pounding as he probed her mouth with his, his arms reaching out to anchor her against his body. Desire flooded every part of her, making an ache grow between her thighs as the kiss grew in intensity. He tasted of a sweet wine; he smelled of both sandalwood and woodsmoke, a masculine scent that was intoxicating, that made her want him even more.

Kisses with men in her own time had been nothing compared to this; a tsunami of pleasure and need that held her captive. She wound her arms around his neck, pressing herself closer to him as he continued to dominate her mouth with his own, their bodies pressed so tightly together that she could feel his heartbeat thundering in tandem with her own. His hands gripped her hair, tilting her head back so he could gain even more access to her mouth, and she let out a wanton moan, her senses aflame for him.

When they finally broke apart for air, Astrid's heart continued to thunder, her desire continued to rage.

Domhnall looked down at her, his eyes a storm of passion before he stood, swallowing hard as he looked away from her.

"Come. I'll escort ye back tae yer chamber."

IT WAS difficult for her to sleep that night, dark thoughts of her parents and her raging need for Domhnall pulling her in two different directions. The kiss had inflamed her ache for Domhnall even more, and it hurt her that he regretted kissing her again; she could see it in his eyes. He'd not spoken to her as he'd escorted her back to her chamber, avoiding her eyes the entire time.

But he was right to regret it. A romantic entanglement between the two of them would be a bad idea; they had a vital mission to accomplish together, one in which lives were at stake.

She pushed the image of Domhnall's handsome face out of her mind as her eyes drifted shut, willing tumultuous thoughts from her mind as fatigue finally claimed her.

She awoke moments later with a start. She had difficulty breathing as if there were a great weight pressing down on her. There was a sense of looming darkness growing within her; it felt like she was standing on railroad tracks watching an oncoming train, and she was powerless to move.

She stumbled out of bed, closing her eyes. Trying to calm her breathing, she murmured a Seeking spell, one that could conjure visions of impending doom.

"*Thoir na seallaidhean a-mach thugam.*"

Almost as soon as she uttered the words, a series of images flooded her mind's eye.

A boat approaching. A view of Farraige Castle from the ocean. A firgure cloaked in shadow. Darkness descending over Barra Isle. Approaching. *Approaching soon.*

Astrid's eyes flew open, and she stumbled to her window to look out at the churning waters beyond the castle walls. She could see nothing but darkness, a blanket of stars, a hovering moon. But something told her that what she'd just seen was coming very, very soon. *Tonight.*

She hastily put on a cloak over her nightdress and tore out of her room, making her way to Domhnall's chamber. She rapped furiously on it until he answered, his tunic wrinkled as if he'd hastily put it on. He frowned down at her, his blue eyes filled with both concern and confusion.

"Astrid, what—"

"I just had a vision of a ship approaching this castle. But not in the future. *Now, Domhnall.*"

$\mathcal{D}$omhnall stood in tense silence on the ramparts of Farraige Castle as he looked out at the surrounding waters; Ruarc and his other men hovered around him. Below, he could see several of his men patrolling the shore that surrounded the castle. Astrid stood behind him and his men; he could feel her watchful gaze on his back.

After she'd told him what she'd seen in her vision, he'd immediately sent for Ruarc and called for his men; his instinct told him to trust Astrid's word.

And now as he kept watch with his men, her presence somewhat eased the tension that gripped him. He didn't know what it was about her that made him feel comforted by her presence even in light of a looming threat.

He hadn't wanted her to come to the ramparts with him and his men, worried for her safety, but she'd insisted. He was now glad that she was here, though he knew his men were curious as to why; many of them kept giving her curious looks. He hadn't explained her presence, but he was prepared with an excuse of her being a healer there to help administer aid should any of them need it.

He clenched his fists at his sides as he looked out at the surrounding waters, wondering with trepidation if the Norse were about to launch a surprise attack. Ulf had told him that his Norse allies were still preparing for their onslaught, sending out raids for now as opposed to an all-out invasion until they regained their strength, as they were still weakened from the recent war.

But was Ulf lying to him? Did he know what was about to happen?

Domhnall's anxiety spiked as he continued to wait in watchful silence with his men, a silence only periodically broken by the patrol guards he'd sent to monitor activity of the immediate surroundings. But their updates were benign; there were no sightings of the Norse nor any intruders in the vicinity.

The watchful sojourn seemed to stretch for hours, with Domhnall not moving a muscle, his hand continually straying to the hilt of his sword, his gaze sweeping over the surroundings, never letting his guard down for a moment. He sensed the growing restlessness of the men around him, even Ruarc, who he knew trusted Astrid's ability. He'd only told them a spy had tipped him off to a possible nighttime invasion; only he and Ruarc knew that he was relying upon Astrid's magic.

As the time stretched his watchful tension did not ease; something in him told him he needed to heed Astrid's warning.

Yet when he saw a boat approaching in the distance, panic still thrummed through his veins despite his tense preparedness. Around him, his well-trained men immediately took up offensive positions, spreading out along the ramparts.

Domhnall stiffened as he studied the distant vessel. He'd seen many ships approaching these shores during the war, but this wasn't the deter-mined approach of a vessel with the intent to attack. It was much smaller than a ship designed for battle, likely capable of only transporting a dozen men. And it remained resolutely in the distance as if it were trying to avoid being seen.

This wasn't the movement of a vessel about to attack.

"Domhnall." Ruarc's voice at his side was urgent. "Shall we ready for an attack?"

"No," Domhnall said, his eyes still trained firmly on the vessel. "We wait."

A ripple of surprise sounded among his men.

"My laird," Ruarc said tightly, reverting to his formal title, something he only did when he was trying to rein in his anger. "A vessel is approaching—"

"It isnae approaching; it lingers in the distance.

I'll nae have needless bloodshed," Domhnall snapped. "We. Wait."

He leveled Ruarc with a hard look before turning to face his other men. "Ye're all tae stand down until I say otherwise."

Ruarc's jaw tightened, but he gave him a jerky nod. His men still looked baffled and uncertain, but they lowered their weapons.

Unable to stop himself, Domhnall turned to give Astrid a brief look. She offered a nod of her head, showing that she agreed with him. This gave him more confidence than he was willing to admit, and he turned his gaze back to the vessel in the distance, his heart thundering.

Tension gripped him as he and his men kept their gazes on the vessel. It continued to keep its distance, hovering for what seemed like an eternity before it turned and drifted away, until it became a speck on the horizon.

Only then did Domhnall allow himself to breathe.

"I donnae understand," Ruarc said, his brow knitted together in a confused frown.

"It may have been a spy ship," Domhnall said, thinking out loud. "Perhaps testing our defenses—I donnae ken. But I intend tae find out."

He turned to his men, ordering them to maintain their posts and to switch shifts as needed for the rest of the night.

"I'll stay up here with the men," Ruarc offered.

"No. I'll stay. Ye get back tae yer wife," Domhnall said. Ruarc looked as if he would refuse, but at Domhnall's firm look, he obliged.

"I'm staying tae keep watch with my men," Domhnall said in a low voice, approaching Astrid once Ruarc left the ramparts. "I'll escort ye tae yer chamber."

"Maybe I should stay up here," Astrid said after a hesitant pause.

"Ye've already done yer part in warning me. It will do ye no good tae remain out here in the cold. My men are well-trained in case of a surprise attack. If I have need of ye, I will send for ye."

Astrid gave him a reluctant nod, taking his extended hand as he guided her off of the ramparts. A warmth encircled him at her touch, a warmth he allowed himself to relish in.

"How did ye ken that a ship would approach?" he asked as they descended the narrow staircase back into the castle. He'd been in such a panic when she'd told him of her vision that he hadn't pushed her for details.

"I saw it in my mind's eye. It was . . . hazy, like something you'd see in a dream. But most of all, I felt a foreboding. It's as if my magic wanted me to sense the danger more than anything."

Amazement swept over him; he didn't know if he would ever get used to her ability to perform such feats. He'd been a fool to nearly turn away such power.

"Astrid," he said, once they reached her chamber, "what ye can do . . . 'tis truly a gift. I cannae apologize enough for nearly turning ye away, for threatening ye with the dungeons."

"You've already apologized, and I understand why you reacted that way," Astrid said, giving him a reassuring smile. "And what I can do . . . it doesn't feel like a gift. It never has. It feels like a curse. I'm not a saint, Domhnall. You forget that I'm only here because my magic tortured me with visions. I would have ignored it if I could have."

"But ye didnae," he said, unable to stop himself from reaching out to touch her face. "Ye didnae, and ye came tae this time. Ye didnae even return tae yer own time when I threatened ye with the dungeons. That says much about ye."

"You think too much of me."

"I think that ye think tae little of yerself, lass."

As her eyes locked with his, her beauty causing a flare of heat to sear his insides, it took everything in his power to not claim those lips of hers with his own once more. It would be so easy to lean down, to wrap his arms around her, to—

"My laird, the patrol guards have a question for ye."

The voice of one of his men behind him jerked him from his desire-tinged reverie, and he dropped his hand from Astrid's face.

"I'll be up shortly," he said, his eyes still locked with Astrid's.

There was fierce longing in her eyes, longing that made him want to take her hand and drag her

into her chamber, to claim more than just her lips—
to claim her body as well.

"I bid ye good night, lass," he ground out, quelling
his ache for her as he made himself walk away.

AT MIDDAY THE NEXT DAY, Domhnall was on a
boat to Leagh Isle to meet with Ulf.

The night before, after Domhnall had left
Astrid's chamber, he'd stayed on the ramparts most
of the night with his men until it was clear that the
boat wasn't returning.

He'd barely slept, only going to his chamber
just before dawn broke, giving orders to his spies to
find out what they could about the mysterious ship.
Thinking of the ship now, Domhnall had to quell
his anger, praying that his cousin wasn't behind it.

Ulf was waiting inside the cottage that served
as their meeting place, warming his hands over the
hearth's fire. He turned, offering Domhnall a wide
smile as he strode inside, but it faded when he saw
the look of fury on his cousin's face.

"Cousin," Ulf said with a frown. "What ires
you?"

"Why was there a Norse ship hovering off the
coast of my isle last night?"

Ulf's eyes widened in surprise. Domhnall
studied him closely; there was no hint of deceit in
his expression. He looked genuinely taken aback.

"I know nothing about a ship coming to your isle," Ulf said with a fierce scowl. "We've had several ships go to some surrounding isles to test defenses. I've told my allies that you're one of us, Barra is to be left alone."

Domhnall continued to study his cousin, still not detecting any deceit. His anger ebbed, replaced by that familiar guilt when Ulf stepped forward and placed his hand on his shoulder.

"I swear to you, I'd never betray you. You're my blood."

Domhnall had to look away at his words, a sharp reminder that he himself was doing just that. He strode away from his cousin to look down at the blazing fire in the hearth.

"Ye didnae mention they were already testing defenses."

"It was only recently decided," Ulf said, a dark look of excitement on his face. "There's to be a large coordinated raid on three of the weakest isles, to take place in a fortnight. The Scots won't have time to fight back. Once we've reclaimed those isles, we can go after our remaining lands."

Dread spiraled through Domhnall as he struggled to keep his expression neutral. *Ye must do whatever it takes tae stop this,* he told himself.

He faced his cousin, forcing a wicked smile as he met Ulf's eyes, hating himself for the lie he was about to speak. "Which isles? I want tae ken which lands I can claim for my own."

CHAPTER 11

strid dismounted from her horse and approached Fyfa's cottage, nervous anticipation coursing through her veins. She'd come alone this time, determined to at least get Fyfa to hear her out.

The door to the cottage was open, and as she approached, she could hear wheezing. Her medical instincts took over, eclipsing her nervousness, and she entered.

The interior of the cottage was modest, with a small hearth, table, cookware, and two straw mattresses in the rear. An elderly man lay sprawled out on one of them, a frantic and pale Fyfa at his side, pressing a damp rag to his forehead, murmuring softly beneath her breath. As Astrid drew closer, she realized Fyfa was murmuring Healing spells.

Fyfa stiffened as she looked up to see Astrid.

Her look of panicked fear dissipated, replaced by anger. "What are ye doing in here? Get out."

Astrid ignored her, her gaze straying toward the man. She could now see the resemblance between him and Fyfa—the same sturdy features, the same green eyes. This must be Fyfa's father. She took in his pale face and labored breathing, thinking fast.

"Is his skin hot to the touch? How long has he been breathing like that?"

Fyfa stared at her, her expression mutinous as she seemed to struggle with herself. But her concern for her father must have won out; she turned grave eyes back to him.

"He's been hot tae the touch since yesterday. His breathing became labored this morning."

"I assume you've been using Healing spells?"

"Aye," Fyfa said shortly. "None worked. But none of this is yer concern, I'll—"

"I'm a healer in my time. I can help him," Astrid insisted, stepping forward. "Move him onto his stomach—it'll help his breathing."

Fyfa hesitated, again seeming to battle internally with herself.

"Do you want to save his life?" Astrid snapped, fed up.

Fyfa swallowed, vulnerability flickering across her face. She gave Astrid a curt nod.

"Then help me move him onto his stomach."

Astrid moved forward, and together she and Fyfa gently rolled the man onto his stomach. She knew this would ease the pressure on his lungs and help him breathe. She suspected, based on his symptoms, that he had pneumonia, for which he needed antibiotics. But given that such medicine was still centuries away, she'd have to rely on what she could do for him now, and what was at hand.

"He's going to need fluids—water, hot broth. A lukewarm compress to bring down his fever. Ginger root for his cough and reducing chest pain. And cloves," Astrid said, thinking out loud. "When you have the broth, you need to have him breathe directly over it to help ease his breathing."

"I—I have some broth and water," Fyfa said, getting to her feet. "And some cloves, but nae ginger root."

"I can bring some back from the castle," Astrid said, leaning down to press her head to the man's back to listen to his lungs. She ached for her modern tools—an X-ray or stethoscope, but she had to rely on what she could hear. As the man breathed, she could hear the faint sound of fluid. A sign of inflammation.

Fyfa returned with water and a bowl of hot broth. Astrid propped the man up while Fyfa gently pressed the water to the man's lips, urging him to drink, which he did.

"What's his name?" Astrid asked Fyfa.

"Iurnan," Fyfa said, her worried gaze trained on the man's face.

"Iurnan," Astrid said, addressing the man. He blinked, fatigued eyes settling on her. She gave him a kind smile. "You need to breathe in over this hot broth. It'll help ease your breathing."

"Listen tae her, Father," Fyfa urged. "She's from a time yet tae come."

A jolt of surprise went through Astrid, though she shouldn't have been. Iurnan clearly knew his daughter was a stiuireadh. Beneath the man's haze of fever and fatigue, she could see curiosity and intrigue in his eyes before he dutifully took several deep breaths over the broth.

Gradually, his labored breathing eased, and Fyfa laid him back down after feeding him more broth and water. Astrid stood, moving back to give Fyfa some privacy with her father.

Fyfa leaned over and murmured soothing words Astrid couldn't hear before placing a makeshift compress made of plaid fabric to his forehead. She then stood to approach Astrid, regarding her with wariness, but her previous hostility had dissipated.

"I thank ye," she said grudgingly. "How did ye ken what tae do?"

"Based on his symptoms, I believe he has something called pneumonia." She saw the confusion cross Fyfa's face, and decided not to go into the intricacies of bacterial and viral infections, something that wouldn't be discovered until centuries in the future. "I've treated it before."

Fyfa swallowed hard, once again looking vulnerable. "Will—will he survive?"

"I don't know," Astrid said honestly. "The best

sign will be if his fever goes down—if he's no longer warm to the touch. Keep doing what I advised, and I'll bring back ginger root from the castle, but you should be able to tell in the next day or so."

Fyfa closed her eyes briefly but nodded. When she opened her eyes again, resentment shone in their depths. "I suppose ye'll want my help with other stiuireadh in return for yer help with my father?"

"No," Astrid said as Fyfa's eyes widened with surprise. "I helped him because it was the right thing to do. Despite what you think of me, I'm not evil, and I'm not responsible for what my parents did. I only want to help—to stop what's coming to the people of these isles."

Fyfa held her gaze for a long moment, her expression still hard, saying nothing.

"I just want to meet with other witches," Astrid continued, desperation creeping into her voice in spite of herself. "There was a spy ship off these shores last night; the laird knows an attack is coming. Without our help, more war, more death will come to the isles. All that being said, if you still choose not to help me, fine. I'd still like to check on your father tomorrow."

Fyfa remained silent, and defeat settled over Astrid. She expelled a sharp breath and turned, heading to the door. "I'll be back tomorrow to check on your father."

She was almost at the door when Fyfa's voice stopped her.

"My coven meets nae far from here on an islet off the coast, where we're free tae practice our magic," she said.

Astrid turned, hope blooming in her chest. Fyfa gave her a shadow of a smile.

"Ye can come with me tae the next gathering."

~

ASTRID RETURNED TO THE CASTLE, eager to tell Domhnall that she'd finally made progress with Fyfa.

As she made her way up the stairs to get to his chamber, a willowy brunette intercepted her. Astrid remembered her as the woman who'd given her a death glare the first night she'd come to the great hall, after she'd told Domhnall she intended to stay.

Forcing a polite smile, Astrid tried to move around her, but the woman blocked her path.

"I donnae ken who ye are, but ye should ken that the laird always returns tae my bed," the woman hissed.

Astrid stilled, stunned by the gravity of the jealousy that tore through her. "I don't care what your relationship is with the laird," she lied, leveling her with a hard look. "I'm here as a healer and nothing more."

The woman looked pleased at this, her lips curving into a threatening smile. "Make certain it stays that way. The laird will one day be my husband." She held Astrid's gaze before stepping back to let her proceed up the stairs.

As Astrid continued up the stairs, her need to see Domhnall dissipated. Her chest felt tight with acrid jealousy, jealousy she had no right to feel. Of course Domhnall would have a mistress—many mistresses. The man was gorgeous. Their kisses were mistakes that shouldn't have happened; she didn't have a claim on him.

She returned to her chamber, the woman's words echoing in her mind. Were they lovers still? Was she telling the truth? Did Domhnall intend to marry her? Were they already engaged?

Astrid told the chambermaid who came to clean her chamber that she would take her supper here instead of in the great hall. She knew she was being childish; she had to see Domhnall at some point to tell him about her meeting with Fyfa's coven; she just didn't trust herself to not show her hurt when she saw him.

But her attempt at avoiding him failed; he entered her chamber a couple of hours later as she sat on the floor, mentally reviewing spells.

He looked breathtakingly handsome as always, his deep-blue belted tunic accentuating his muscular form, the color of the tunic highlighting the blues of his eyes.

"Yer chambermaid tells me ye wish tae take yer meal in yer room. Are ye well? Did Fyfa still nae agree tae help ye?"

"No, she agreed," Astrid said, getting to her

feet. She tried to keep her tone neutral. "She'll take me to their next meeting."

Domhnall smiled, and it was difficult to not get caught up in that smile. Heat spiraled in her belly, and she averted her gaze.

"Then what's wrong?" he pressed.

Astrid briefly debated against telling him about the brunette, but decided it was best to get it over with. "I bumped into your mistress. She warned me away from you," she said finally.

There was a tense silence as Astrid waited, hating herself for hoping he would deny having a mistress. When she finally raised her eyes to meet his, they were thunderous with anger.

"What did she look like? This lass who claimed to be a mistress?"

Relief tore through her at his words; the tension ebbing from her body. By the look of angry disbelief in his eyes, the woman was most certainly not his mistress.

"Tall, brown hair, dark eyes. Bonnie," she added, another misplaced shard of jealousy piercing her.

"Moirna," he muttered, his scowl deepening. "I'll have words with her. She likely thought she could talk tae ye so because her uncle is a noble. I apologize, ye shouldnae have tae deal with such matters when ye're only here tae help."

"It's fine," she said quickly—too quickly. "It's none of my business, anyway."

He stared at her for a long moment and took a

step closer, causing a heated awareness to spread throughout her body. "Ye didnae take tae heart what she said, did ye?"

"No," Astrid said. "And, really, it's none of my business."

She stared stubbornly at his broad chest, refusing to look up at him, until he reached out and tilted her head up.

"Moirna is bonnie, aye. But ye should ken, I want ye more than I've ever wanted her . . . more than I've ever wanted any lass."

Her heart picked up its pace as his gaze darkened with lust. He reached out a thumb to stroke her bottom lip, the act so erotic that she couldn't stop the shudder that swept over her.

"Ye're beautiful, Astrid," he murmured. "The most beautiful lass I've ever seen."

Her pulse pounded wildly as he leaned down to claim her mouth with his. Winding his arms around her, he walked with her backward until she was pressed against the far wall. Electricity sizzled through her veins as he reached down to hike up her gown, continuing to dominate her mouth with his.

Astrid moaned against his mouth, her body overcome with arousal as Domhnall continued to lift up her gown until it was gathered at her waist. She tore her lips away from him, flushed with surprise as he lowered his fingers to stroke her heated center.

"Domhnall," she gasped as he continued to

stroke his finger in and out of her, causing a fierce desire to claim her senses.

Astrid was quivering, barely able to breathe. He kept his blue eyes trained on hers, leaning forward to again seize her mouth once more as his finger kept up its deliberate strokes.

"Aye, lass," he murmured against her mouth as she could feel the beginnings of her orgasm, a delicious ache stirring between her thighs. "Come for me, lass. Let me see ye fall apart for me."

His words, his kiss, his masculine beauty, and the insistence of his fingers against her center caused her pleasure to build to a crescendo. Astrid threw her head back, letting out a cry as her orgasm claimed her.

He kept probing her mouth with his as she quaked, forcing her to moan her desire into his mouth, until he finally released her.

Had he not held her up she would have collapsed. He continued to hold her as she caught her breath, his lips against her hair, his heartbeat thundering along with hers.

"I ache for ye, lass, though I ken I shouldnae. Moirna nor any other lass compares tae ye, my bonnie witch. Donnae forget that."

CHAPTER 12

omhnall had to force himself to leave Astrid's chamber. He shouldn't have allowed himself to touch her so, but he was losing the battle against his desire.

Perhaps he'd lost it the very moment he laid eyes on her.

He kept his determined strides until he reached his own chamber, where he leaned against the wall, waiting for his arousal to ebb, for the image of Astrid's lovely face, flush with passionate intensity as her climax claimed her, still fresh in his mind's eye. He stood there for what seemed like an eternity before he moved over to the window where he rubbed his temples.

Now that he'd had a taste of Astrid and touched her so intimately, witnessing how beautiful she looked when she succumbed to her pleasure, he didn't know how he was going to set aside his need for her. And now that he knew the Norse were planning to invade several nearby isles imminently, he needed every ounce of his focus.

He'd already arranged to meet with the chieftain of the clan to the north of Barra, Neacal, the next day, and dispatched his messenger Aodh to warn the other lairds of the isles the Norse were targeting.

He'd promised Astrid that she could come with him to his meeting with Neacal. Now he regretted this. With the magnitude of his desire and protectiveness toward Astrid, how could he keep focus during the meeting if she was there?

This is yer own doing, he admonished himself. *Ye never should have allowed yourself tae touch her.*

Tearing his thoughts away from the distracting witch, he made his way to the great hall, now relieved that Astrid had insisted on having her meal in her chamber. It would be difficult to resist her pull if she were in the hall with him. He was doing a poor job of concealing his longing for her if Moirna had recognized her as a potential threat.

It was not long after he took his seat at the head table that Moirna approached, wearing a gown of deep sapphire that may have once caught his eye. But now, she might as well have worn rags compared to Astrid and anything the bonnie witch wore that clung to her beautiful body.

"My laird," Moirna purred, dipping low to ensure that he had an unobstructed view of her milky bosom. "I've nae seen ye in some time. I was hoping tae share a meal with ye."

"I'm certain there are a great deal of men who wish tae seek yer acquaintance," he said shortly, recalling how hurt Astrid had looked as she recounted her interaction with Moirna.

Moirna paled, her smile faltering. "My—my laird—"

"There is a foreign lass, Astrid, staying here as my guest," he said, leaning forward and lowering his voice. He noticed that their exchange was drawing attention from the other guests. "Ye insulted her, which means ye insulted me. After tonight's feast, I no longer wish tae see ye here at the castle."

Moirna went even more pale, opening her mouth as if to protest, but stopping at the hard look in Domhnall's eyes. She swallowed and gave him a shaky nod before turning to leave him.

"I confess I never liked Moirna," Ruarc murmured. Domhnall startled; he'd not noticed his friend take the seat at his side. "But banishing her from the castle? Her uncle will nae be happy with ye."

"Senan answers tae me, he'll nae interfere. His niece stepped out of line when she insulted Astrid," Domhnall said, terse. "I'll nae have a former mistress insulting my guests."

"Is that all that Astrid is?" Ruarc asked, his voice taking on a teasing tone. "A guest?"

Domhnall met Ruarc's eyes. His friend gave him a knowing grin, and Domhnall quickly looked away.

"Aye," he said, knowing that the words were a lie even as he spoke them. "She's here tae help us with our defenses against the Norse, and nothing more."

~

THE NEXT DAY, Domhnall entered the great hall of Castle Laidirh, with Ruarc and two of his top nobles flanking him.

Astrid trailed them, her head bowed and covered with a hooded cloak. Again, her presence brought him that familiar sense of calm, a calm that had eased his anxiety during the journey to Castle Laidirh from his lands.

The great hall was filled with a handful of Clan Lairdirh's nobles, who all regarded him with guarded wariness. Neacal sat seated at the center of them, his dark eyes unreadable.

"I received yer message, Laird Flachnan," Neacal said, leaning back in his chair. "How do I ken what ye say is truth?"

"Because I have no reason tae lie," Domhnall said evenly, tamping down his anger at the subtle accusation. "I share this isle with ye. I want it and the people who dwell here tae be safe."

"Ye have Norse kin. How do we ken ye're nae working with them?" a gray-haired noble at Neacal's side asked, his green eyes narrowed.

The nobles mumbled in agreement. Domhnall tensed, but forced himself to remain calm. "We fought alongside each other against the Norse," he reminded Neacal. "If I wanted tae betray my own men, my clan, then that would have been the time. But I've bled alongside all of ye here. Barra is my home, and I will fight for my home."

"Or perhaps ye are weary of fighting the Norse after the last war, and ye're now fighting alongside them?" the same noble at Neacal's side hissed, glaring at Domhnall. "Perhaps ye're luring us intae a trap?"

More grumbles of agreement erupted from the men, but Domhnall kept his gaze on Neacal. Neacal's face was a stoic mask.

Domhnall expelled a sigh. He knew he wasn't going to get anywhere with his men shouting baseless accusations. "My laird," Domhnall said, focusing on Neacal, even as the nobles continued to rumble. "May I speak tae ye alone?"

"Our laird doesnae need tae—" the noble began.

"Enough, Cathal," Neacal said firmly, cutting off the man with a hard look. "I will speak tae the laird alone and then send for ye."

Cathal stiffened but grudgingly got to his feet. The nobles filed out of the hall, including Ruarc and Domhnall's nobles.

But when Astrid started to leave, Domhnall stopped her. He needed her counsel; he suspected she could read Neacal in ways that he couldn't.

"Stay," he said gently, taking her arm.

Cathal, who had nearly reached the door, took

notice of this. He whirled back around, stalking toward them with a scowl. "Why does yer whore get tae stay and—"

All thoughts of peace and diplomacy vanished as white-hot anger blazed a fiery trail through Domhnall's gut. He reached out, grabbing Cathal by the collar of his tunic and lifted him bodily off the ground. Astrid let out a cry of surprise and protest, and Neacal's men immediately went into offensive stances.

"Astrid is nae a whore. She's a spy who is risking her life tae help the Scots," he said through clenched teeth. "She is my guest and under my protection. Ye will apologize tae her."

"Domhnall," Ruarc said urgently, "please, put the—"

"Apologize," Domhnall growled, his entire focus on Cathal, who looked terrified as he met Domhnall's furious gaze.

"I—I apologize tae ye, lass," he said gruffly, cutting a quick look to Astrid. "I meant no offense."

Only then did Domhnall release him. Cathal looked at Neacal, red-faced, as if waiting for his laird to interject on his behalf, but Neacal's face remained a stoic mask. Cathal shot both Domhnall and Astrid a dark look before hurrying out of the hall.

Once they were alone, Domhnall stepped forward, his gaze focused on Neacal with intensity. "My cousin is one of the Norse who's launching these attacks. I've pretended tae be on his side, betraying my own kin tae protect my people. That is how ye ken I'm telling the truth. I assume ye're a man of honor, and that is why what I've just told ye willnae leave this hall."

Neacal didn't respond. Instead, his eyes flitted to Astrid, filling Domhnall with unease.

"Who are ye, lass?" he asked.

"She's a spy," Domhnall answered for her, trying not to show his panic nor his prick of jealousy at Neacal's attentions on her.

"No, she isnae," Neacal said calmly, not taking his eyes off of Astrid. "And I assume the lass can speak for herself."

Astrid stepped forward, but Domhnall moved to stand in front of her.

"She is here as my trusted spy, and I willnae have ye—"

"Domhnall," Astrid said from behind him. "It's all right."

He noticed with a chill that Neacal didn't react to her strange accent.

"Again, lass," Neacal said. "Who are ye?"

"The laird spoke the truth," Astrid said stiffly. "I'm a spy who—"

"If we are tae be allies, we need tae be truthful with each other," Neacal snapped, getting to his feet.

His protective instinct flared to life, and Domhnall again moved in front of Astrid, his hand flying to the hilt of his sword. Alliance be damned, he'd not let Neacal harm her.

Neacal scowled at Domhnall, holding his hands up to show he meant no harm.

"I am a man of honor. I would never harm a lass," he hissed. He focused his attention back to Astrid, who had, Domhnall noted with irritation, again stepped out from behind him. "I will ask ye a different question, and this is one I hope ye will answer truthfully."

"All right," Astrid said, her voice level, but Domhnall noticed how she paled.

Neacal held her gaze for a long moment before speaking again.

"What year are ye from, lass?"

CHAPTER 13

Astrid sank down into the chair by the fireplace in Domhnall's chamber, reeling. Behind her, Domhnall paced the length of the chamber, raking his hand through his hair.

"I cannae believe it," Domhnall breathed.

"Neither can I," Astrid returned, shaking her head as she recalled what they'd just discovered from Neacal.

"My mother was a stiuireadh. A fiosaiche," Neacal had told them, his eyes intent on Astrid. "She told me I would one day meet one of yer kind; she didnae tell me how or why. But as soon as I saw ye . . . I kent there was something different about ye. I sensed it."

"Then you know how important it is that we work together. My magic guided me to this time to help stop what's coming," Astrid had said, when she could finally work past her shock.

She'd told him of the Pact and of the version of

history she knew. Neacal had listened intently, his brow knitted, before agreeing to work with them. But only after Domhnall made him promise to keep Astrid's true identity a secret, which he had, looking offended that they'd assumed otherwise.

Though relieved that they had an ally, they'd left Neacal's castle reeling with the revelation that Neacal knew about Astrid's true identity.

Now Astrid expelled a breath, gazing into the leaping flames of the fire. Domhnall had told her that Neacal was Siomha's cousin. Given that magic often ran through bloodlines, it made sense he would have a close relative who was a witch and would know about the stiuireadh.

"It makes me wonder how many other leaders of the isles already ken about the stiuireadh," Domhnall said, pulling her from her maelstrom of thoughts. "Should I have kent?"

"No," Astrid said, getting to her feet, approaching him with a vigorous shake of her head. "Only a small percentage of people know of the stiuireadh even in my time. And these are still dangerous times for witches, it's better that people know as little as possible."

Domhnall looked relieved at this, tension visibly ebbing from his shoulders. "'Tis good that he kens, that we have him on our side."

"It is," Astrid said, trying to tamp down her anxiety over yet another person knowing of her true identity to focus on the positive. "And Domhnall, I know it's not my place to say this, but maybe it wasn't wise to threaten one of his nobles. Maybe you should have just let him think I was your personal whore. Even though Neacal knows about me, the more I stay in the background for now, the more we—"

Domhnall interrupted her with a growl, glowering down at her. "Ye are nae a whore," he snapped. "And ye willnae call yourself that."

Astrid flushed, meeting his eyes. He looked fiercely possessive, his blue eyes flashing with heat as he met her eyes. A thrill coursed through her at this, and she struggled to keep her voice even. "I know I'm not," she said. "I just think—"

"Not even for show," he interrupted. "Ye're more than that. If my men—if other men—think ye're just a whore, nae only will they nae show ye respect, but they'll want ye for their own."

A ripple of delight swept over her at the obvious jealousy in his eyes. He took a step closer, forcing Astrid to tilt her head back to look up at him. Desire at his proximity claimed her, fierce and hot, sending jolts of awareness throughout her body.

"I ken I have no right tae ye, lass. But I feel possessive of ye. As if ye were mine."

Warmth flared within Astrid as her breath hitched. In that moment, she realized how much she wanted to be his . . . and how much she wanted him to be hers.

Domhnall reached out, taking her gently by the nape before pressing his lips to hers. The warmth within her transformed into the heat of an aching need. She opened her mouth as his tongue explored hers, moisture seeping from between her thighs as the kiss deepened.

Domhnall let out a sexy groan as he trailed kisses down her jawline to her throat, then lower, to the hem of her bodice. He raised his eyes to meet hers before yanking down the bodice and taking a nipple into his mouth, causing her to arch toward him and gasp at the delicious sensations that claimed her.

"Lass," he gasped, releasing her nipple and looking at her with raw hunger. "If ye want me tae stop, tell me now."

Astrid locked eyes with Domhnall, knowing that she should tell him to stop. But that would have been akin to forcing herself not to breathe.

"Please," she whispered. "Don't stop . . ."

Domhnall let out a strangled groan, lifting her into his arms and crossing to the bed. But he didn't deposit her there, instead setting her down on her feet, his hungry gaze raking over her.

"I want tae disrobe ye," he rasped, "tae see the body I've ached tae claim ever since I discovered ye on that shore."

Her pulse began to race at his words, her breathing growing ragged as Domhnall stripped her of her gown, then her underdress, his eyes taking in every inch of her. She flushed at his intense appraisal, her heart beating a furious staccato rhythm in her chest.

"My witch from the sea. Sea witch. *Bana bhuidseach mara,*" he murmured, using the Gaelic word for "sea witch," his eyes lifting to meet hers. "Ye're lovelier than I dreamed."

He kissed her again, holding her naked body so close that it seemed as if their hearts beat in tandem. She moaned into his mouth, allowing her heady pleasure to take hold, to consume her.

When he released her, Astrid reached out to disrobe him of his tunic; her mouth watering at the sight of his muscular chest, gleaming in the firelight. He stepped out of his breeches, and Astrid swallowed as she took in the glorious size of him, standing proud and erect. He was even more gorgeous than she'd allowed herself to believe, and a heated anticipation swept over her.

He gave her a wicked grin as he devoured her mouth once more, reaching out to grasp her by the buttocks as he pulled her in close. He released her, only to sink down to the floor before her as if in worship, raising his eyes to meet hers.

"Look at me, sea witch," he commanded. "Look at me while I taste you."

She obeyed, letting out a ragged moan as his mouth clamped on to her center. The feel of his tongue probing inside her caused a glorious ache to seize her entire body, and tendrils of pleasure coiled around her, causing her to whimper and quake, until her legs could no longer hold her upright and she fell back onto the bed.

Domhnall remained clamped on to her center,

humming against her as he continued to feast. Astrid writhed and gripped the sheets as her pleasure became too much to bear, and it built to a crescendo until her climax claimed her, finally giving her a glorious release. Domhnall remained between her thighs, continuing to lap at her as her tremors subsided.

Only when she stilled did he lift himself above her, kissing her jaw, down to her breasts, again laving each breast until tendrils of pleasure once again coiled around every part of her.

"Domhnall," she gasped, arching toward him. "Please..."

He gave her another devilish grin as he positioned his body above hers. "I confess I do like it when ye beg, sea witch," he rasped. "What do ye want?"

"You," she moaned, not caring how desperate and wanton she sounded. She just needed him, all of him. "I want you, Domhnall. Plea—"

Before she could finish her plea, Domhnall sank inside her and she gasped, moaning at the delicious feel of him inside her.

When he began to move, thrusting with firm but gentle force, Astrid wrapped her legs around him. Their eyes locked as they moved together, and Astrid was once again swept up in a torrent of pleasure. He felt perfect inside her, their bodies moving together in a sensuous rhythm. Domhnall reached out to grasp her hands with his as she threw her head back and moaned, wanting this sense of completeness, of pleasure, to never end.

"Look at me," Domhnall commanded, and she did, taking in his masculine beauty, at the blue eyes that were trained so intently on hers. "Ye're so verrae bonnie, my sea witch. And ye feel as if ye were made for me."

His words caused a burst of joy to explode inside her belly, and as her eyes searched his, seeing the depth of need and desire in them, a revelation struck her.

She was falling in love with him.

It was as if her body awakened to this realization, and another climax shook her. She started to throw her head back to let out another cry, but Domhnall reached out to hold her head still, making her meet his eyes as her orgasm tore through her. He kept his eyes on hers as his own climax claimed him.

Astrid watched hungrily as he let out a guttural moan of pleasure; it was a beautiful sight to watch the man she was falling for succumb to desire, desire he felt for her.

When they both stilled, Domhnall remained inside her, his arms wrapped securely around her, as they both caught their breath. After a moment, he slid out of her, leaving her with an almost painful feeling of emptiness.

He reached for her, and Astrid burrowed herself into his arms, aching to still be near him. Domhnall smiled, reaching out to stroke her face.

"Ye've bewitched me, lass," he murmured.

"Are you sure you're not a witch? Because I think it's the other way around," Astrid returned.

He let out a light chuckle before his smile faded, his hand dropping. "Ye told me ye've no husband. But . . . ye're nae a virgin."

There was no mistaking the jealousy in his voice. Astrid couldn't help but smile; no other man could ever hold a candle to Domhnall.

"I've had a couple of boyfriends in my time," she said. "But I didn't want them nearly as much as I do you." *Nor did I have the depth of feelings I have for you*, she added silently.

Domhnall's scowl only deepened. Astrid chuckled, delighted at his possessiveness. "At least you didn't have any former lover of mine taunt you," she said, her smile fading and her own jealousy spiking as she thought of Moirna.

Domhnall's scowl disappeared, his expression turning contrite. "I told ye she's nothing compared tae ye," he murmured. "My sea witch, ye enchant me in a way that no other lass has—or will."

Or will. Her heart clenched at his words, a stark reminder that her time here with him was temporary, that she was falling for a man who lived centuries in time behind her. A sudden, sharp pain pierced her at the thought of returning to a time where Domhnall Flachnan didn't exist.

"Astrid?" Domhnall asked, sitting up and frowning with concern at the change in her expression. "What is it?"

I'm falling for you, and I can't bear thinking about living in a time where you don't exist.

But she wasn't going to tell him that. As far as he knew, she desired him and nothing more. She wasn't going to complicate things further by confessing her growing feelings for him.

She took a breath, closing her eyes briefly to force the painful thought of Domhnall's lack of existence in her time to the back of her mind. Despite her feelings, she needed to remember why she was here in the first place.

"What if I fail?" she whispered, deciding to focus on something else that worried her, something that had nothing to do with her feelings for him. "What if I don't unite the witches and lairds, and history changes? What if the Norse return and this time they succeed?"

Domhnall's face softened. "Before I became laird, I was terrified of failing in my duty tae the clan. When I told my father of my fears, he told me it was my fear which would ensure my failure."

At Astrid's look of confusion, he continued, "He was right. It was my fear that was leading me toward failure, making me focus on my self-doubt. Once I just focused on the task of becoming the best leader I could, I was able tae defeat my fear."

"You've always known you were going to be

laird. I turned my back on magic. I only came here because—"

"Ye came here tae help because ye're a good person, and as I've told ye before, stronger than ye realize."

He held her gaze, his blue eyes so intense that warmth once again enveloped her. How did he have so much confidence in her? Maybe his unwavering belief in her was one of the reasons she was falling for him.

"Your father sounds like he was a wise man," Astrid said finally, shifting her gaze away from his penetrating stare as if looking away would shield her feelings.

"He was," Domhnall said, his voice heavy with grief.

"What was he like?" Astrid asked, hungry to learn more about his family, to know more about the man she was falling in love with.

Domhnall held her close as he told her more about his father, a stern but kind man who had raised him with a firm hand, and his Norse mother, whom he'd gotten his coloring from, how loving yet fierce she'd been.

And Domhnall listened intently as she told him about her uncle, her heart clenching in grief as she recalled the man who had taken on the parental role in her life, who'd shown her love and normalcy after the darkness of her childhood.

"Ye and I are similar," Domhnall mused, stroking her hair. "Ye've been torn between life as a stiuireadh and a life without magic. I've been torn over loyalty between my Norse and Gaelic sides."

"I was never torn—I wanted no part of being a witch," Astrid protested. "Your Norse and Gaelic ancestry—it's who you are, Domhnall."

"And a witch is who ye are," Domhnall returned, giving her a gentle smile. "I struggle over loyalty tae my Norse kin, but I donnae deny that being Norse is also in my blood. I accept it. I think ye'll find peace by accepting that ye're a stiuireadh."

Astrid wanted to protest, but considered his words. Wasn't she hundreds of years in the past, something she had used her magic to do? Wasn't it possible to be both—a doctor who appreciated science, and a witch who practiced magic? Both sounded incongruous, but they were both what she was. Magic was in her blood whether she wanted to accept it or not.

Perhaps Domhnall was right. If she stopped fighting the magical side of her, she would find peace, and it would make her more likely to succeed in what she'd come to this time to do.

"I must confess, sea witch," Domhnall said, bringing her back to the present, his voice turning husky as he leaned in close. He brushed his lips along the base of her throat, causing sparks of awareness to dance along her skin. "I enjoy both yer magic and non-magical side."

"Do you?" she asked, letting out a soft whimper as he nibbled at her flesh.

"Aye," he growled, lifting his gorgeous body above hers and giving her a rakish grin. "And yer body is quite bonnie. I need tae worship ye once more."

Astrid let out a moan of pleasure as he proceeded to do just that.

CHAPTER 14

A multitude of emotions coursed through Astrid as she followed Fyfa toward a grove of trees.

It was just after midday the next day, and Fyfa had kept to her word, using a Transport spell to take her to the islet where her coven met.

Though she was nervous about meeting with Fyfa's coven, memories of the night before flooded every corner of her mind. Her body still throbbed with pleasure as she recalled Domhnall's hands and mouth worshiping her body, how he'd taken her two more times, bringing her to glorious climaxes each time.

As much as she'd enjoyed their lovemaking, she'd loved their quiet moments in between each lovemaking session even more, their voices echoing around the chamber as Astrid spoke more of life in her time, and Domhnall told her of life on Barra. It was an intimacy that went beyond the physical; an intimacy she longed for more of.

Astrid shook her head as if to clear it from thoughts of Domhnall. How was she going to concentrate on the monumental task of convincing a coven from another time to ally with her when she was so distracted? *You have to,* she urged herself. Fyfa had warned her that the witches of her coven may not trust her, that she would do her best to help convince them, but Astrid needed to be prepared.

She glanced over at Fyfa, who she noticed also looked tense with nervousness. She and Fyfa had spoken little during their brief journey here. While Fyfa had slightly warmed to her since she'd helped heal her ailing father, there was still a wariness there. Astrid suspected it would be some time before Fyfa fully opened up to her.

Astrid took in the small islet that surrounded them. It was called Eilean Nan Draoidhean, isle of the druids, in Gaelic. Before they'd left, Fyfa told her the stiuireadh had used this islet for generations; it was a sacred place for their druid ancestors. A large, sandy shoreline snaked around the isle, and lush green groves dominated it. Surrounded by churning waters, there was indeed something magical and otherworldly about it. She could imagine generations of stiuireadh practicing their spells here.

A handful of women and one older man

emerged from a grove of trees as they approached, forcing Astrid back to the present. Nervousness flaring once more in her belly, Astrid halted next to Fyfa. This must be Fyfa's coven, and as Fyfa had predicted, they all stared at her with blatant hostility.

Her gaze landed on one of them—a tall, severe-looking woman with silver-blond hair and slate-gray eyes. An odd sensation pierced Astrid's chest at the sight of her, and she forced her gaze away from the woman's penetrating stare.

Another one of the women, tall, formidable and sharp-eyed with long gray-streaked auburn hair stepped forward, her eyes narrowed.

"Who is this, Fyfa?" she demanded, shooting Astrid a glare. "Ye ken that no one is tae come tae our coven gatherings."

"She is a stiuireadh, like us, Lachina," Fyfa said, ducking her head in submission. "She's come here from another time. There's something urgent she needs tae discuss with ye all."

All of the witches stiffened with surprise, but the suspicion on their faces didn't fade. Lachina froze momentarily before stepping forward, her eyes trailing over Astrid from head to toe with harsh appraisal.

"Are ye from the past or from a time that has yet tae come?"

"A time that has yet to come," Astrid replied, holding her gaze evenly though her heartbeat pounded a frenetic rhythm. Lachina's widened at her modern accent as Astrid continued, "Eight centuries from now."

There was a collective gasp among the witches. Lachina paled, but continued to study her. "And why are ye here?"

"To warn you. Another war will come to these isles, a war that can be prevented if you unite with the lairds of the isles. You know there are Norse who are ignoring the peace treaty and continuing to raid. I'm here to tell you it will only get worse—they'll continue to bring death and destruction to these lands. But they can be stopped, if you join with the leaders of the isles."

The witches looked at her with astonishment, while Lachina's anger seemed to spike; her mouth tightened, and her eyes narrowed. "Things may be different in yer time, but do ye ken how dangerous it would be if we were tae expose ourselves? Some may ken about us, aye, but they pretend tae nae ken of our existence. If others were tae ken—"

"You only have to tell the lairds who will ally with you, and only the ones you believe you can trust," Astrid interrupted, her tone urgent. "If they know harm is coming to their lands, they'll want to ally with us."

"Us?" Lachina echoed, her expression darkening. "We donnae stand with ye—we donnae ken who ye are. How do we ken ye speak the truth? How do we nae ken ye've come from another coven that wishes tae destroy us?"

"She isnae."

To Astrid's surprise, it was Fyfa who spoke up, and all eyes turned to her.

"I was suspicious of her at first, but I've foreseen her arrival in this time. She's working with one of the lairds of Barra, Laird Domhnall Flachnan. He is a good man; he trusts her. I think that speaks tae her nature. And she helped my ailing father when she didnae have tae. I believe she speaks truth."

Astrid gave Fyfa a grateful look. But Lachina said nothing, continuing to glower at Astrid. She abruptly stepped forward, reaching out to take Astrid's hand. The move was so sudden that Astrid started to jerk away in surprise, but Lachina held firm as she murmured the words of a spell in Old Gaelic that Astrid didn't recognize.

Lachina closed her eyes, holding still for several long moments, until she dropped Astrid's hand as if she'd just been burned and stumbled back, her eyes wide with horror.

"I see darkness in yer line," she breathed. "Ye have kin that are aingidh?"

"My parents were aingidh," Astrid replied, not breaking eye contact even as that old feeling of shame twisted inside her. "But I'm not like them. I'm only here to help."

It was as if she hadn't spoken. Now the witches were muttering among themselves, looking at her with blatant distrust, while Lachina whirled to face Fyfa.

"Get this aingidh off of our isle," she hissed as Fyfa stumbled backward, looking pale-faced and stricken. "If ye ever bring her tae me again, I'll release ye from the coven."

"Please," Astrid said, desperation rising as she stepped forward. She'd been prepared for some pushback from other witches, but not this level of hostility. "I only want to—"

Astrid let out a startled cry as an invisible force lifted her bodily off of her feet as a spell struck her in the chest, slamming her onto the ground with such force that the air seemed to whoosh out of her entire body.

Lachina stalked toward Astrid as she lay on the ground, reeling, her eyes narrowed into slits.

"Leave now, aingidh, or I'll submerge ye in the sea until ye drown."

~

"Ye need tae do something tae earn Lachina's trust," Fyfa said.

Astrid and Fyfa were making their way back to Fyfa's cottage from the shore of Barra. Astrid was going to do a brief follow-up medical check on Fyfa's father, who was now in full recovery from his illness. But she was distracted, still stricken over Lachina's fury and her magical attack.

How can I get the witches to trust me if they don't see past my bloodline? What if history changes for the worse because I can't convince them to make the Pact that can save the isles from more warfare? What will happen to Domhnall? His people?

Fear rose in her belly, mingling with panic, and she closed her eyes, trying to focus on Fyfa's words. "How?" Astrid asked warily, rubbing her temples. "She hates me—as you did."

"I never hated ye," Fyfa corrected. "I just didnae trust ye. Yer help with my father made me trust ye."

"I don't know how to earn her trust. I have no doubt she'll try to kill me if I approach her again."

"Nae if ye approach her somewhere where she cannae harm ye," Fyfa said, turning to face her.

Astrid studied her, baffled. She'd half expected Fyfa to refuse to help her after Lachina threatened to release her from the coven. Though not as vital in her time, covens were helpful to witches for a sense of community; it was a magical family of sorts. Yet Fyfa seemed even more determined to help her now.

"I believe what ye say about the Norse," Fyfa said as if reading her thoughts. "I donnae want more warfare tae come tae the isles."

"And where—how—can I approach her without her killing me?" Astrid asked, shivering as she recalled the anger in Lachina's eyes; the force of her power.

"Lachina is more than just a stiuireadh," Fyfa said, giving her a smile that was almost mischievous. "Come inside, and after ye've checked in on my father, I'll make ye a warm broth before ye return tae the castle. I'll tell ye who Lachina truly is."

CHAPTER 15

*D*omhnall rode his horse across the broad expanse of Barra, Ruarc at his side, taking in the defenses that both his and Neacal's men had arranged. Together, they'd made certain they had men manning the small ports that dotted the isle, and additional men at lookout posts at various spots along Barra's extensive coastline.

All morning, it had been difficult to remove thoughts of his bonnie sea witch from his mind. He kept recalling the delicious feel of her body, how soft her skin was, how desirable she'd looked beneath him, her dark curls spread around her like a halo as he'd taken her. He'd made love to her twice more during the night, and he still wasn't sated. He wanted more of her. Needed more of her.

It had been difficult to leave her side after dawn broke; he'd wanted nothing more than to spend the day in bed with her, learning everything there was to know about her, a need that he admitted to himself went beyond desire. He had left her only after a long, lingering kiss that he'd made himself end as he would have taken her to bed again had he not done so.

"Domhnall?" Ruarc asked, forcing him back to the present.

"Aye?"

"The northern part of the isle looks secure; we should check the southern coastline once more," Ruarc said, studying him closely. "Are ye well? Ye seem—"

"I'm well," he said shortly, not wanting Ruarc to know what had him so distracted. "Aye, let's check the southern coastline."

But as he started to turn his horse, a rider approached him and Ruarc from the south, moving at a quick speed. Domhnall stiffened with panic and reached for the hilt of his sword, his alarm only quelling when he saw it was Aodh, his personal messenger.

"My laird," Aodh said as he approached, his face pale with panic. "There's been an attack on Muck Isle tae the east. 'Tis the Norse. Farms burned. Men killed."

AFTER HE AND Ruarc arrived back at the castle, Domhnall made his way to the great hall, anger and frustration rising within him. Ulf had said nothing about an attack on Muck. According to Aodh, the other isles Ulf had told him of remained unharmed.

Did Ulf not know about this attack? Unease settled over him as he realized this was unlikely. What if his cousin had told him of a false attack against the other isles as a test of his loyalty? Had his cousin realized his betrayal?

As much as he dreaded it, he needed to see his cousin to find out the truth. But first he would meet with his men to make certain they were prepared for a potential surprise attack.

He recalled the dark days of the war against the Norse: the constant battles, the defenses he and his men struggled to maintain against the determined Norse, the injuries and deaths among his men, the toll of constant battle on the men and women of Barra—people he was supposed to protect.

And now he was failing at preventing yet another war.

He clenched his fists at his sides, tamping down his anger and frustration. Just as he and Ruarc reached the doors to the great hall, Astrid hurried toward him from the opposite end of the corridor. Warmth, desire, and something foreign swept over him at the sight of her, but he tapped the emotions away, like extinguishing a burgeoning flame. He had to force coldness into his gaze, his body. His yearning for Astrid had made him lose focus; while he'd worshipped her body the night before, the Norse were planning to launch yet another attack, on an isle not far from Barra. He couldn't risk her distracting him again.

"Domhnall—" she began.

"I have a meeting with my nobles. There's been a Norse attack on an isle just east of here," he said shortly.

Astrid blanched at this, horror flitting across her lovely features, and he had to quell the urge to comfort her, keeping his gaze hard.

"Did ye get other stiuireadh tae join ye?"

"N—no," Astrid said, still looking shaken. "But—"

"I will talk with ye later after I speak with the nobles," he interrupted, forcing himself to move past her.

"Should—should I come in with you? Maybe I can—"

"No. There's nothing ye can do," he said, hating himself for both his forced coldness and his need to take her in his arms, to reassure her.

Instead, he avoided looking at her altogether as he entered the great hall, Ruarc right behind him.

"Was it necessary tae talk tae her so harshly?" Ruarc asked in a low voice.

"There's just been an attack on an isle nae far from here. I can talk tae the lass later," Domhnall said shortly.

Ruarc's mouth tightened, but he seemed to know better than to argue.

The meeting with his nobles was brief; they looked as shaken as he was about the attack on

Muck; some had family who resided there. Nobles from Muck had helped Barra with food and supplies during the last war with the Norse; they had proven to be loyal allies.

"We will send what aid we can spare, provide those whose farms were burned with staples and water," Domhnall told his men. "We also need tae strengthen our own defenses. I want men on boats patrolling the eastern and western coasts of Barra."

"And what of yer cousin?" asked Larragh, one of the older nobles who had served his father, his brows knit together in a frown. "He told ye the attacks were tae take place on other isles."

"I will deal with my cousin," Domhnall said, both fear and anger roiling through him at the thought of Ulf betraying him. "But for now, we must do all we can tae assure that our lands are secure."

After his men had left the hall, Domhnall turned to Ruarc. "I need tae see my cousin—tonight," he said brusquely.

"I agree that ye need tae speak with Ulf, but ye need tae practice caution. Bring yer most trusted men as guards with ye."

Domhnall gritted his teeth. He still wanted to hold on to hope that Ulf hadn't purposely misled him, that his cousin trusted him even while Domhnall deceived him.

But he couldn't allow himself such naïveté. He needed to prepare himself for Ulf's wrath. His heart twisted in his chest, and he gave Ruarc a curt nod.

❧

HE TRAVELED to Leagh that evening with several guards, his blood racing with grim anticipation. He knew it would take some time for Aodh to reach Ulf in Orkney with the message that he wanted to meet; he was prepared to spend the night at the cottage that served as his and Ulf's meeting place. He tried not to think of how he'd spent the previous night, wrapped around Astrid's beautiful body.

He entered the cottage, expecting to find it empty, but he froze in surprise. Ulf stood there, his arms crossed over his shoulders, his expression hard. And unlike the other times they'd met, two men flanked him. Two Norsemen.

Domhnall's guards instantly went into a defensive stance. Domhnall held up his hand for calm, though his heart pounded with alarm.

"My allies didn't truly believe you were with us," Ulf spat, glaring at him. "They wanted me to test you by telling you of a false attack to see if anyone was warned, when in truth they were planning to raid Muck. And they were right. You betrayed me, cousin."

His voice broke, and for a moment Ulf's rage dissipated; he looked as Domhnall had remembered him as a lad. Vulnerable. And now, heartbroken.

Guilt surged in Domhnall's chest, and he opened his mouth to defend himself. Yet before he could, Ulf strode across the room, pressing the blade of his sword to his throat. Panic flared to life within Domhnall as Ulf's men forced Domhnall's guards back.

"We are blood, yet you choose the Scots. I should cut you down," Ulf hissed.

Fear laced through Domhnall, yet he didn't show it. He held his cousin's gaze and spoke the truth. "I did what I did for peace. For my people."

"Until we get our lands back, there can be no peace," Ulf snarled.

Several tense moments passed, moments that seemed like an eternity as Ulf remained still, a tumult of emotions fluttering across his face, his blade against Domhnall's throat.

He finally lowered his sword and stepped back, giving Domhnall a look of such hatred that it was like a physical blow.

"I told my allies I would kill you for your betrayal. Because you are my blood, I will show you the loyalty you didn't show me and spare your life. But you will stay out of this fight, cousin. Or I swear to you, when I see you again, I *will* strike you down."

CHAPTER 16

Astrid entered her chamber, blinking back tears of hurt, reeling over Domhnall's coldness. Unlike last night, he'd treated her like a distant stranger. Pain splintered her chest as she thought of the disregard in his eyes; it was as if their shared intimacy the night before hadn't happened.

Was Domhnall upset with her? Did he regret what occurred between them?

The thought pained her even more, and she closed her eyes. If he regretted their lovemaking, maybe he was right to do so. The recent strike by the Norse only proved the danger was increasing, and she still hadn't accomplished what she'd come to this time to do.

Moving over to the window and looking out at the surrounding ocean, she recalled what Fyfa had told her about Lachina.

"She's the wife of a high-ranking clan noble; Manus. Only her husband kens who she truly is. If ye go see her at her home, she cannae use magic against ye; it will risk revealing who she is. But ye'll have tae ken what ye'll say tae convince her. I donnae think ye'll have another chance after that."

Fear tightened Astrid's belly at the thought of approaching Lachina once more. By the force of her spell, Astrid could tell Lachina was a powerful witch, and Astrid was still struggling to grasp her own power.

But she had no choice. She needed to get the witches to unite with the lairds as a defense sooner rather than later or risk history being completely rewritten.

Her determination renewed, she ignored her lingering heartbreak as best she could for the rest of the day, remaining in her chamber to mentally review and practice spells, but not before telling the chambermaid that she would again take supper in her chamber. She was too hurt and embarrassed to face Domhnall in the great hall, though some part of her hoped he would come to see her and apologize.

Before she ate dinner, she went to Siomha's chamber to perform a medical check, something she'd made a mental note to do periodically as long as she was in this time. Pregnancy was especially risky in this time, and if she could help Siomha's pregnancy go smoother, it was the least she could do even if she didn't have modern equipment.

Siomha greeted her with a warm smile when she entered, allowing Astrid to press her hand to her belly to feel for the baby's heartbeat, patiently answering Astrid's questions about fatigue, her appetite, and other pregnancy-related symptoms. Based on Siomha's answers, and the solid pounding of the baby's heartbeat, Astrid could tell that it was a healthy pregnancy.

A surprising rush of envy coursed through her when she pressed her hand to Siomha's belly. In her own time, Astrid hadn't given too much thought to children as she'd never met anyone she wanted to raise a child with. Now, she couldn't help but imagine a child of hers and Domhnall's, with her dark curls and Domhnall's sharp blue eyes. Domhnall, with his sense of honor and duty, would make a wonderful father.

"Astrid?" Siomha was asking.

Astrid blinked up at Siomha.

"Are ye unwell? Ye looked far away for a moment."

"I'm fine," Astrid said hastily. "Everything seems healthy with your pregnancy and the baby."

"Will ye stay with me for a meal?" Siomha asked as Astrid straightened. "Ruarc has a meeting with the laird and the other nobles, and I'm curious tae learn more about this future ye come from."

"Of course," Astrid said, returning her smile, though another stab of pain pierced her over Domhnall not including her in this meeting. He seemed determined to avoid her.

She forced her thoughts away from Domhnall as the chambermaid brought her and Siomha a meal of roasted herring, bread, and vegetables, setting it up on a table before the fireplace.

It was good to spend time with someone with magical ability who wasn't so hostile to her like Lachina. Though Fyfa seemed to no longer harbor any ill will toward her, Siomha was the only one with magical ability in this time who'd treated her with kindness from the start.

After Astrid told her of her tense encounter with Lachina, Siomha gave her a sympathetic look, leaning back in her chair.

"Ah, Lachina," Siomha said with a sigh. "I ken her well. I ken she was harsh tae ye, but she has a good heart. She's only protective of her coven and doesnae trust strangers."

"She threatened to kill me," Astrid said, unable to keep the harshness from her tone. "That goes beyond mistrust."

"Aye," Siomha said, giving her a nod of agreement. "But ye must understand, 'tis dangerous in this time tae have magic, though some ken of us. There are those who wouldnae hesitate tae kill one of our kind; they fear the ability of the stiuireadh."

A chill coursed through Astrid at her words; they were a stark reminder of just how dangerous this time was for witches.

"I understand. I guess the force of her hostility took me by surprise. This all has been more difficult than I thought. And then there's Dom—" She stopped herself, flushing. She felt so comfortable with Siomha that she'd almost confessed her feelings for Domhnall.

"Ye care for the laird," Siomha said, studying her closely. It wasn't a question but a statement of fact.

Astrid opened her mouth to protest, but no words came. There was something so genuine and open about Siomha that she couldn't bear to lie to her.

"Yes," she admitted. "But—nothing can happen," she added, tactfully deciding not to mention their night of lovemaking. "We both have duties to tend to. And . . . I'm from a different time."

"Love is more powerful than time," Siomha said, waving her hand with dismissal. "It is more powerful than our own will. I didnae intend tae love Ruarc. I was born in my cousin Neacal's clan, which was once an enemy of this clan's. Had love obeyed what I wanted, I would have married someone from my own clan. Nae falling for Ruarc was like fighting against the pull of the ocean's waves. I had no choice but tae give in tae its pull."

Astrid nodded as Siomha's words permeated. Her growing love for Domhnall did indeed feel like a gravitational pull.

"Speaking of your cousin Neacal, he knew who I was, and that I wasn't from this time," she said, wanting to change the subject from her feelings for Domhnall.

"I should have warned ye before ye went tae

see him. My cousin may nae have the Sight, but he is insightful. His mother was a stiuireadh. I take it that's why he agreed tae ally with ye?"

"Yes," Astrid said, relieved that Siomha didn't press to learn more about her and Domhnall.

"I'm glad. My cousin can be stubborn, but he is a good man."

Siomha began to pepper her with questions about the future. Astrid smiled at her inquisitiveness, and gave her an overview of life in the twenty-first century, telling her about the significant populations and cities, America, and technology.

As she spoke of the time in which she was born, Astrid realized she didn't miss it as much as she thought she would. True, there were the modern conveniences she'd taken for granted, but life in a medieval castle was comfortable, especially given that she had her own servants, meals were provided, and Barra was uncommonly beautiful. And despite the ongoing threat of conflict with the Norse, there was a sense of quiet calm that was missing in her modern-day life in Los Angeles.

She was attempting to explain to Siomha what driving was like—something else she also didn't miss in traffic-clogged Los Angeles—when Ruarc entered the chamber. He gave Astrid a polite nod before turning to give Siomha a look filled with such love that she couldn't help but feel a wave of envy as she recalled how cold Domhnall behaved toward her earlier. How good would it feel for Domhnall to look at her like that?

Setting her envy aside, she bade them a good night and left Siomha's chamber.

Her feet seemed to have a mind of their own, taking her to Domhnall's chamber instead of her own. She told herself she wanted to know what occurred at the meeting he'd had with the nobles, though deep down she knew better—she just wanted to see him.

Domhnall's chamber door was open; he stood by the fireplace, looking down into the flames, his brow furrowed. Astrid's heart leapt at the sight of him, her thoughts returning to the night before as she'd hungrily taken in Domhnall's muscular torso gleaming in the same firelight.

When he looked up at her she swallowed, fearful that he'd tell her to leave with that same coldness he'd displayed earlier, but he gestured for her to enter.

"My cousin Ulf now kens of my true loyalties," he said, a look of both grief and frustration flickering across his handsome face. "We've increased the defenses around Barra, and we'll send what aid we can tae the Isle of Muck. Ye mentioned that the other stiuireadh didnae want tae join ye?"

She shouldn't have felt so upset by his curt tone, but she did. It was like she'd imagined the night they'd shared. The night she realized she was falling in love with him.

"The coven leader, Lachina, was . . . hostile," she said, hoping that her voice sounded formal, not echoing the deep longing she felt for him. "She used a spell against me and threatened to kill me if I approached her again."

Domhnall's expression went from tense anxiety to concern—and anger. It reminded her of how he'd looked at her when he found her on the shore, with a fierce protectiveness.

He strode across the chamber toward her, taking her arm with a frown. Electricity jolted through her at his touch, recalling how his hands had glided along her arms as he'd thrust into her the night before.

"I ken Lachina—I didnae ken she was a stiuireadh. Ye're bruised," he added with a growl. "Did she do this tae ye?"

She followed his gaze, noticing for the first time the slight bruise that had formed on her arm from landing on her side after Lachina's magical attack.

"It's nothing," she said, unnerved by his anger. "I'm more upset about the fact that she refused to help than—"

"'Tis nae all right. Ye'll nae approach her again."

"I have to talk to her again, Domhnall. According to Fyfa, she's trusted among the covens of the isles. They'll listen to her."

"Then I'll come with ye," he said without hesitation. "I may nae have magic, but I'll have words with her about harming ye."

A wave of pleasure swept over her at his protectiveness; it was a stark contrast to his coldness. His expression softened, and he lifted his hand as if he was going to touch the side of her face, but he dropped it.

"I want tae apologize tae ye, lass," he said gruffly. "I shouldnae have been so cold tae ye earlier. I was worried about the latest attack."

"I understand," Astrid said, lowering her gaze. "You don't have to apologize."

"I do," Domhnall insisted. "Ye must ken how much I want ye. How I care for ye . . . more than I should. But after the attack on Muck, I need tae focus on my duties. And being with ye . . . making love tae ye will make it difficult for me tae do so."

Each word he spoke was like a sledgehammer to her heart; it took everything in her power to evenly hold his gaze, to nod in agreement, to not act as if her heart wasn't breaking in her chest.

"You're right. I think that's for the best. Last night shouldn't have happened," she forced herself to say.

An emotion she couldn't identify flickered across his face at her words, and he opened his mouth, but Astrid couldn't bear to hear any more rejection, any more words that would pierce her heart. She turned and hurried out of his chamber, an ache searing her chest.

CHAPTER 17

*E*arly the next morning, Domhnall stood at Astrid's side at the front door of the manor home Lachina shared with her husband, Manus.

He'd had a sleepless night, regretting his words to her as soon as they'd spoken them. He'd wanted to chase after Astrid and beg for her forgiveness, to tell her that he couldn't stay away from her after the night they shared, but he'd forced himself to let her go.

When they'd met at the stables to make the journey to Lachina's home, Astrid had barely acknowledged him, only giving him a polite nod. Her distance had stung him more than he'd antici-pated; he now understood how Astrid must have felt when he was cold to her.

"L—Laird Flachnan," a servant stammered as she opened the door, looking astonished at the sight of him. "The laird of the manor isnae here, I'll—"

"We're here tae see Lachina," Domhnall said firmly.

The servant widened her eyes in surprise, her gaze sweeping to Astrid before she nodded and took a step back, gesturing for them to enter.

She led them into a sizeable drawing room; they were only there for a moment when Lachina entered, a pleasant smile on her face, one that faded as soon as she saw Astrid.

"Laird Flachnan," Lachina said, her voice tight as she turned to look at him. "My husband isnae—"

"I'm here tae see ye," he interrupted. "There's no need for formalities. I ken what Astrid is, and what ye are. She only wants tae help ye. Ye had no right tae harm her."

Lachina stiffened, shooting Astrid another withering glare before responding. "My laird, she is kin of aingidh. It wouldnae be wise tae trust her."

"I trust her," Domhnall growled. "Are ye calling me a fool?"

"N—no, my laird," Lachina said. "I just—"

"I only want to help," Astrid interrupted, stepping forward. "There was just an attack on Muck by the Norse. It's only a matter of time before they come here."

"The Norse have always raided the isles," Lachina said, though her voice wavered with uncertainty. "And I have a fiosaiche in my coven. She's foreseen no such danger. No such alliance."

"Well, I'm from the future, and I'm telling you, there is one. But the future isn't fixed—the Norse can still bring death and destruction to the isles. If we work together, the future where there is peace can remain intact. I've seen darkness coming, and it's happening soon. You need to tell the other stiuireadh that we must work with the lairds to stop the Norse."

"Ye'll nae issue me orders, aingidh," Lachina hissed.

"Donnae speak tae her in such a manner," Domhnall snapped, his patience fraying. Guilt filled him as he recalled how he'd treated Astrid similarly when she'd arrived—with distrust and hostility.

Astrid turned to give him a placating look as if to say, *Let me handle this.* His mouth tightened and he obliged her. But if Lachina uttered one more word against her . . .

He watched, tense, as Astrid stepped toward Lachina, determination stark on her lovely features.

"What are ye—" Lachina began, her body stiffening with alarm.

Astrid didn't respond, grabbing Lachina's arm and murmuring several words beneath her breath; Domhnall suspected they were words of a spell.

Lachina went still with shock, her eyes going wide as Astrid released her. She stumbled to her knees, pressing her hands to her temples as Astrid stepped back.

"What did ye do?" he asked Astrid, astonished.

"Showed her what I've seen. What made me

come to this time," Astrid grimly replied, not taking her eyes off of Lachina.

It took several moments, but Lachina soon stopped trembling, climbing to her feet, still looking pale.

"If we don't work together to stop the Norse, *that* is what will happen," Astrid snapped. "Think of your fellow stiuireadh, your fellow men and women. You know what I speak is true, you know what I've just showed you is true. I can't plant false visions in the mind of another stiuireadh."

Lachina closed her eyes. When she opened them, she gave Astrid a grim nod. Though there was still simmering contempt in her gaze, there was also a grudging respect. "I will talk tae the other coven leaders," she whispered. "Ye have my word."

~

"How WERE ye able tae put visions in her mind?" Domhnall asked in amazement after they'd returned to the castle.

Despite her success in getting Lachina's assistance, Astrid had remained silent during the entire journey back to the castle and even while he'd accompanied her back to her chamber. He noticed that Astrid still took great care to keep distance between them, something that tore at him. He hoped his question would force her to open up to him.

It is ye who told her ye need tae keep yer distance, he reminded himself with a stab of regret.

"It was a complex Seeking spell, one I didn't think I'd be able to pull off, but I think my desperation helped," Astrid said, still not looking at him.

"What did ye see in yer visions? The ones that compelled ye tae come tae this time?" he asked, determined to keep her talking to him.

"They were . . . flashes of images. I saw ships on water, battles on land. I saw women weeping over dead bodies, crying children, bloodied bodies on fields. Images of warfare," she said, a shadow passing across her features.

At her words, a chill crept up his spine. He thought of the recent war with the Norse, the bloody battles, the death, the despair. Dread filled him at the thought of such events once again coming to pass.

"I think what I showed Lachina has convinced her," Astrid continued, moving to the window of her chamber, her expression carefully blank. "She'll keep to her word. Getting the coven leaders to work together is a step in the right direction. Once they're working together, there won't be any need for me here. She and the other witches are more powerful than I am. I—I think once I unite them with the lairds, I've done what I came here to do. My magic will leave me be, and I can return to my own time."

"No," Domhnall said before he could stop himself, panic spiraling through him at the thought of her leaving. He knew she would eventually have to leave, but he wasn't yet ready.

He didn't think he'd ever be ready.

Distance be damned, he thought, crossing the chamber to stand before her. She looked up at him, her lovely green eyes widening at the intensity in his own.

"Ye need tae stay and see the Pact through, Astrid. Ye need tae ensure that the Pact brings peace tae the isles. I believe ye're still needed here."

He was trying to prolong her stay, but he believed every word. Gazing down at her bonnie face, he ached to take her into his arms, to claim her mouth and body once more. To tell her that despite what he'd said about keeping their distance, he couldn't bear to see her go.

"I'll consider it," Astrid said, turning away from him, her expression shuttering. "I'm going to practice some spells. If you need me, I'll be here."

It was a dismissal, one he was tempted to disregard. But he told himself he deserved her coldness after he'd pushed her away. She was doing what he'd asked her to do.

Still, it took everything in his power to turn on his heel and leave her chamber. *I do need ye, Astrid,* he thought, as he closed the door behind him. *More than ye ken.*

CHAPTER 18

It was easy for Astrid to keep her distance from Domhnall over the course of the next couple of weeks as she ventured with Lachina to both the islet where the local coven met, Eilean Nan Draoidhean, and several other nearby isles, meeting with leaders of other covens to convince them to work with the lairds. She knew that Domhnall himself was busy working with Neacal, approaching the other lairds of the isles to warn them of another invasion by the Norse and forging alliances.

She ached for him, and missed him more than she should, even as she tried to focus on the task at hand. *If I miss him this much when we're in the same time,* Astrid silently despaired, *how will I cope when we're centuries apart?*

But she forced her heartache aside to focus on what she'd come here to do, something that Lachina was vital in helping accomplish.

There were three main covens operating throughout the isles, with several dozen members in total. The largest coven was on the Isle of Skye, another on Barra, and another on Benbecula. Fyfa told her that each coven operated like a clan, with fierce loyalties within each, and bitter rivalries with other covens, often going back generations.

It was only during the war with the Norse that they truly came together, though they'd ultimately decided to not get involved; it was a war involving men and men only, and they hadn't wanted to risk exposing themselves. Astrid knew that this would make it even more difficult to convince them to join with the lairds in fighting off the Norse, but she could only hope that Lachina could convince them otherwise.

Before each meeting, Lachina curtly ordered Astrid to remain silent and let her do the talking, warning her that the other coven leaders were even more distrustful than she was.

Lachina hadn't warmed toward Astrid at all; it seemed as if she barely tolerated her. If it weren't for Domhnall and the visions she'd put in her mind, Astrid was certain Lachina would have made good on her promise to drown her.

Two other witches from Lachina's coven would accompany them to meet with the coven leaders, one of them being the silver-haired witch who had given Astrid that odd, dark feeling. Every time the witch's gaze passed over Astrid, a shiver coursed through her. There was something off about the witch, something she couldn't quite place. When she asked Fyfa about the witch, she told her the witch's name was Erskina.

"She's from an ancient line of druid witches and she's especially powerful. Donnae fret how she behaves; she's nae friendly toward anyone in our coven except for Lachina," Fyfa informed her.

Astrid made herself dismiss the odd feeling she had about Erskina, telling herself that it must just be because of the cold, suspicious air Erskina gave off whenever she looked at Astrid.

While Lachina remained cold, and Erskina and the other witches regarded her with lingering suspicion, Fyfa had fully warmed up to her. She learned that Fyfa's grandparents were stiuireadh, but her parents possessed no magic. Her father kept what she could do secret; Siomha was one of the few in the clan who knew of her power.

"'Tis another reason I was so cold toward ye. I didnae want many people kenning of my magic. It can be dangerous for people tae ken," Fyfa said, giving her an apologetic look.

"I understand," Astrid said, offering her a warm smile in return.

Fyfa's former hostility aside, she was grateful that Fyfa accompanied her and Lachina to each meeting with the coven leaders; it was nice to have a friendly witch with her. While Lachina spoke to the witches privately, Fyfa would take Astrid aside and help her practice both Offensive and Defensive spells.

At first, Astrid's magic stubbornly refused to comply, but toward the end of the first week she could issue several Defensive and Offensive spells with ease. In her own time, Astrid had ignored her magic, but at times could feel it prickling beneath her skin as if it were fighting to get out. Now, as she allowed her magic to flow freely throughout her body, she realized what a mistake it had been to restrain her magic. She shouldn't have let her parents' dark actions plague her for so long. It felt exhilarating to allow her magic to course through her without restraint.

"Yer power has always been there, 'tis yer fear that's held ye back. Let go of that fear and allow yer magic tae take hold," Fyfa urged.

"Even though there are aingidh in my blood-line?" Astrid asked, that old fear and shame seizing her.

"Aye. I was wrong tae judge ye harshly. I now ken that ye're a good lass. Ye only want tae do what's right."

"The other witches still don't trust me," Astrid muttered, frustration surging through her.

"They will, with time," Fyfa assured her, but Astrid wasn't so certain.

After days of Lachina meeting with the leaders, it was a cool yet sunny afternoon on the Isle of Skye when Lachina approached her, along with several coven leaders. Astrid, who had been practicing Defensive spells with Fyfa, stilled as they approached, her heart picking up its pace.

"They wish tae hear what ye have tae say—from yer own lips," Lachina said stiffly, looking unhappy about this.

Astrid turned to face the witches, who regarded her with looks ranging from curiosity to mild suspicion. One of them, a petite brunette with warm yet intense brown eyes who looked Astrid's age, stepped forward.

"Tell us of these visions ye've seen in yer time."

Astrid recounted the visions that had tortured her in her own time, and the witch listened intently.

"I believe ye," the brunette witch said when Astrid fell silent, her expression grim. "The fiosaiche in my coven has sensed darkness coming."

Lachina looked surprised by this, giving her a frown. "Why did ye say nothing about this when I first approached ye?"

"I wanted tae see the stiuireadh who told ye of this darkness for myself. I kent ye said she is kin of aingidh, but I see no darkness in her. I think she speaks truth."

"As do I," said another leader, a tall man with auburn hair and deep brown eyes.

"And I," said another, an elderly woman who gave Astrid a nod.

Soon there were murmurings of agreement among all the coven leaders. Astrid watched, tense with hopeful anticipation, as they stepped back from her and spoke among themselves.

It was then that she realized just how much she

wanted this all to work out—how much she truly cared that the Pact took its rightful place in magical history. At first, she'd just wanted to heed her magic's call and get back to her normal life. Now that she'd developed feelings for Domhnall, she wanted to do whatever she could to keep him and his people safe.

Finally, Lachina emerged from the group, addressing Astrid. "The leaders are in agreement. As long as we can get assurance from the lairds, a vow, that they will keep our secret and protect us as well, we will ally with them tae stop the Norse from reclaiming the isles."

CHAPTER 19

"The stiuireadh have agreed to work with the lairds. They just want assurances that the lairds will keep their identity a secret."

Domhnall studied Astrid, who hovered by his chamber doorway, her eyes averted. He couldn't help but drink her in; the past fortnight had been torture keeping his distance from her. He'd ached for any glimpse he got of her, and at night his body throbbed with need for her, memories of their love-making flooding his mind.

As much as he desired her body, he mostly missed just being in her presence. Her laughter, the musical lilt of her voice, her alluring beauty. He hated that she barely looked at him; even now, her eyes were trained on anywhere but him. *Ye did this,* he cursed himself. *Ye're the fool who pushed her away.*

He had to force himself to focus on her words, a

rush of relief filling him as they settled in. He and Neacal had been busy forging alliances with the other lairds of the isles; they now had most on their side. The recent war with the Norse was fresh in the minds of the other lairds; they knew it was impossible to fight off such a determined enemy without alliances.

"I believe Neacal and I can convince the lairds tae agree; they ken we need all the help we can get tae fight the Norse. I've been telling them of a powerful ally tae prepare them for learning of the stiuireadh." He paused, wishing she would just look at him, but her gaze was carefully trained on some spot behind him. "I thank ye, Astrid. I ken it wasnae easy given that many witches in this time donnae trust ye."

She gave him a stiff nod. "I just wanted you to know. Ah—have a good evening."

She turned to leave, but he crossed his chamber in several long strides, reaching out to grip her arm, turning her to face him. Her startled green eyes met his, her alluring lavender scent teasing his nostrils. In that moment he wanted nothing more than to lift her into his arms, to carry her to his bed, to never let her go.

"Donnae do that, lass," he said roughly.

"Do what?"

"Close yourself off tae me. Yer smiles . . . they're like the sun. Donnae shield them from me."

Astrid blinked up at him in surprise. "You're the one who said we needed to keep our—"

"I ken what I said," he growled. "And it was foolish of me. I never should have said it."

"But you—you were right," Astrid hedged, struggling to get out of his grip, but he held firm. "We have to focus, we have to—"

"Tell me, Astrid," he growled, stepping so close to her that their bodies touched, gritting his teeth against the wave of arousal that coursed over him, "have ye been able tae focus this past fortnight? Because I havenae. I awake tae thoughts of ye, lass. I go tae sleep thinking of ye. My ache for ye has only grown, my bonnie witch from the sea. I've scarcely been able tae breathe without ye at my side."

When Astrid's eyes locked with his, he saw yearning lurking in their green depths. She didn't have to say a word for him to know that she felt the same.

It was all he needed.

He leaned down, claiming her luscious mouth with his. Astrid moaned as he explored her sweet mouth, his need for her rising and making his cock stir. He kicked the chamber door shut and guided her back to the bed, her body pressed to his as if they were entangled in an erotic dance.

When they reached the bed, he set her down on his lap, winding his hand through her dark curls, continuing to dominate her mouth with his. When he finally released her for air, her lips were swollen from his kisses, her face flushed. A possessive thrill snaked through him. He was the one who had made her look like that. His desirable witch. His bonnie Astrid.

"Thoughts of ye consume me, and they have ever since ye washed up on that shore. I thought that by keeping my distance I could stop thinking of ye, but it has only made me long for ye more."

"Domhnall," she whispered, her eyes filling with emotion. "I want you too. So much."

Her words caused his desire to spike, and he seized her mouth once more.

"I'm afeared," he rasped, releasing her mouth to pepper kisses along her jaw and down her throat, to the curve of her delectable bosom, "that I cannae restrain my desire for ye."

She gasped as he hiked up her gown and adjusted himself to lower his breeches, reaching down to stroke her soaked center. He placed his fingers into his mouth, tasting her sweetness, letting out a low grumble.

"Ye taste like honey, sea witch," he murmured, keeping his eyes locked on hers as he settled her onto his aching cock.

Astrid let out a cry of pleasure, and he moaned at the delicious feel of her tightness clenched around him. He reached out to grip the nape of her neck, forcing her to keep her eyes locked on him as he thrust into her, their bodies moving together in a seductive rhythm.

He gripped her by the buttocks, squeezing her flesh, and she whimpered, her lips parted, sighs and whimpers emitting from her lips. Making love to her was the sweetest pleasure, and he hungrily took in her bonnie body as she rode him, leaning forward to capture a rosy nipple in his mouth.

"Come for me, lass," he rasped against her breast. "Come for me, sweet Astrid."

She obliged, her body shaking as her release claimed her, the sight the most beautiful thing he'd ever seen. Only when she stilled did he allow his own pleasure to take hold of him, and he locked his arms around her, holding her tight as he released himself inside her.

Together, they fell back onto the bed, still trembling and breathless, their hearts thundering in tandem. Domhnall sat up and took her in with his eyes, hunger for her seizing him once more.

"That was for me, sea witch," he murmured, reaching out to touch the side of her face. "This time, 'tis for ye."

"Domhnall," she moaned, as he lowered himself between her thighs, hiking up her gown, leaning down to feast upon her sweetness before he took her once more.

Afterward, once they'd reached another mutual release, they lay together entwined in each other's arms.

He stroked Astrid's hair, a contentment filling him that he'd never felt before, a contentment that went beyond sated lust. It was this contentment, this joy, that lulled him to a peaceful sleep, his arms around his sea witch, feeling as if he'd found his own version of home in her arms.

But when he awoke later, it was to the sound of Astrid's screams.

CHAPTER 20

Joy and contentment settled over Astrid as she lay in Domhnall's arms in the aftermath of their lovemaking.

After his confession of missing her during the past couple of weeks, joy had filled her, chasing away the melancholy that had been her constant companion during their time apart. As they'd talked, she'd allowed herself to fantasize once more about staying here in this time with him, using her medical expertise to tend to the locals, strengthening her magic, even starting a family—having children who wouldn't know darkness, only the light of magic that she'd come to embrace.

It continued to surprise Astrid how little she missed her own time, but ever since her beloved uncle had died, there was only her career and not much else in her life. She had a few acquaintances she liked, and she enjoyed her job, but there had always been a certain emptiness in her life. She felt more fulfilled in this time after falling in love with Domhnall and accepting magic than she ever had in her own time.

But would Domhnall even want her to stay? She knew he desired and cared for her, but did he want her as a permanent part of his life? He'd never even hinted at this, and she needed to accept that it was unlikely. They had come together under extraordinary circumstances, but once things were back to normal, Domhnall would go back to his duties as laird and chieftain, and expect her to go back to her time. Then he could be free to marry someone suitable.

Astrid swallowed back a lump of hurt at the thought, laying her head down on his chest and listening to the steady thrum of his heartbeat. She shouldn't think about the painful time when they'd part ways forever. All that mattered now was making certain that the man she loved and his people were safe.

"I love you, Domhnall," she whispered to his sleeping form, before closing her eyes and allowing his soft breaths to lull her to a peaceful sleep.

She awoke not long after drifting off with a gasp, her heart pummeling against her rib cage, a sense of . . . *wrongness* seizing her. It was a similar feeling to the night she'd had a vision of the Norse ship approaching Barra. But this sensation felt more ominous.

She shifted, looking down at Domhnall's sleeping form. It was still the middle of the night, and she didn't want to cause him undue panic if this was a false alarm.

She quietly slipped out of bed, moving over to the window and pushing it open, taking in a breath of cool night air to calm herself. Yet the sense of urgency remained, her magic prickling restlessly beneath her skin.

Was another boat approaching? Was it another attack?

Taking a breath, she stretched her hands out before her, murmuring the words of a Seeking spell.

"Thoir na seallaidhean a-mach thugam."

She waited patiently, but nothing came to her. She dropped her hands to her sides, wondering if she was just tense and on edge because of the looming conflict with the Norse.

But that dark feeling of premonition lingered. And there was the sense that during her time here, she was still missing something.

Think, Astrid. She went back to her medical school training, recalling a course where she'd learned how to detect a mysterious illness from the symptoms a patient cited. Her professor had taught her to go over any and all clues, even the most mundane.

Using that same method, she thought of everything she'd learned, and sensed, since coming to this time. The images of warfare she'd seen in her vision. That mysterious spy ship. The witches she'd met during the past few weeks.

And that's when a face came to mind. That silver-haired witch, Erskina, who gave her an odd, dark feeling. Perhaps there was something about that witch she was missing.

Keeping the vision of Erskina firmly in her mind, Astrid closed her eyes and uttered the Seeking spell once more.

This time, an onslaught of visions filled her mind's eye.

Erskina screaming over several dead bodies. A house burning to the ground. Rage burning in her gray eyes. Erskina meeting with a group of men she didn't recognize—but based on their Nordic looks, Astrid assumed they were Norsemen. Erskina standing on a boat, Barra in the distance. Erskina standing over flames that were spreading, a dark look of glee in her eyes.

She didn't realize she was screaming until she felt Domhnall's hands on her arms. She met his concerned gaze with tear-filled eyes, her entire body shaking.

"It's Erskina, one of the stiuireadh in Lachina's coven," she whispered, her throat raw. "She's an aingidh . . . and she's working with the Norse."

Everything made sense now. It was why she had that sense of impending doom—an aingidh was in her very midst. One of the first dreams she'd had after arriving in this time had been of a dark figure stalking her from the shadows. And there was that sense of malignant energy she'd gotten from Erskina; she now recognized it as the same feeling she'd had around her parents as they'd succumbed to darkness.

Panic pierced her, fierce and intense. Was Erskina working alone or with a coven of aingidh? How could they defeat them if so? This wasn't something mentioned in her time, only that the stiuireadh worked with the lairds to ward off the Norse. Had something gone differently in the patchwork of time?

She stood and moved to the bed, sinking down heavily onto it. Domhnall, who had gone pale at her words, sat down next to her.

"Ulf didnae tell me this," he muttered.

"Maybe he didn't know, or maybe he was still testing you."

"Are ye certain of this?"

"Yes," she said. She was right about Erskina; she felt it in her bones. It was the final piece to the puzzle that she hadn't realized she was missing. "We need to tell Lachina. And we can't delay any longer with the Pact; we need to get the lairds and witches together to seal it and get our defenses established. Erskina may have sensed that I've figured out what she is."

"Aye," Domhnall agreed, raking his hand through his hair. "But it takes time tae get messengers tae the lairds—sometimes days."

"That's what we have magic for," Astrid replied, thinking of the Transport spell she had recently mastered with Fyfa's help. "But first . . . I have a plan."

❧

Hours later, just before dawn, Astrid, Fyfa, Domhnall, and Ruarc stood on the edge of a glen, eyeing the cottage where Fyfa had told her Erskina lived.

Given the lack of trust that Lachina and the other witches had in her, Astrid knew she needed to get confirmation of Erskina being an aingidh before she approached them with what she knew. Fyfa, Domhnall, and Ruarc were here as eyewitnesses. Siomha had wanted to join them, but Ruarc had wisely refused to allow his pregnant wife anywhere near an aingidh.

Astrid looked at the cottage, her heart hammering. She'd been terrified to confront an aingidh on her own, especially when she'd never engaged in a magical attack before, but Fyfa had performed a Searching spell and confirmed the cottage was empty. Now, all she needed was to find some sort of proof to bring to Lachina.

"Must ye do this on yer own?" Domhnall muttered from behind her. "Surely there are other stiuireadh who can join ye."

"There isn't much time; we just need proof," she said, turning to give him a reassuring smile. "There isn't anyone in the cottage. I'll be fine."

She and Fyfa had mutually decided to go in without Domhnall and Ruarc; as witches, they could hide any lingering trace of their presence in the cottage with a Cloaking spell. It would be more difficult to cloak Domhnall and Ruarc's presence.

Domhnall gave her an abrupt nod, though he still looked on edge, his hand going to the hilt of his sword as if by instinct. She suspected this was a first for him. As laird and chieftain, he was used to doing the battling, the protecting.

But this was her battle.

She nodded to Fyfa, who took her hand, murmured the words of a Transport spell, and she found herself in Erskina's cottage.

She took in the empty cottage; it didn't look like the home of a powerful, dark witch. It was a relatively simple one-room cottage with a straw mattress, a hearth with dying embers, and cookware perched on a table. It was only when she looked closer that she noticed a slight lump beneath the mattress.

Moving over to it, Astrid nudged the mattress with her foot. It slid back, and a chill roiled through her when she saw that a groove was dug out beneath the mattress. Within it were various items: torn-up pieces of clothing, small sacks with clumps of hair stuffed inside, jars of blood, and herbs. All of these items would be vital ingredients for spells, but they weren't proof of dark magic.

"We can't use any of this as proof," Astrid said with a sigh. "We'll just have to go directly to Lachina and pray she believes me."

"No," a cool voice behind them said, making

the hair stand up on Astrid's neck, "ye willnae be doing that."

They whirled, and Astrid froze at the sight of Erskina behind them. She was leaning against the door, smiling at them pleasantly as if they'd just visited her to share a cup of ale.

Panic surged within Astrid. Where had she come from? How had she known they were there? Had she harmed Domhnall and Ruarc?

"I kent ye were from a time yet tae come even before ye told the coven," Erskina said with that eerie smile. "I should have killed ye then. I figured ye were here tae stop me even if ye didnae ken it yet. But I wanted tae see what ye kent."

"I didn't know what you were. Not right away," Astrid said, hoping that talking would buy her time as she frantically thought of spells she could use.

"Why, Erskina?" Fyfa breathed, both pain and fury lacing her tone. "Why are ye betraying yer people?"

"My people?" Erskina hissed, her sudden calm evaporating. "Let me tell ye what 'my people' did. My family were of Norse descent as well as Gael. They lived here in peace for generations until the Scots got greedy and took the land my kin had for generations. We had a fine home they burned tae the ground in the war. Because my family chose tae remain loyal tae the Norse, they lost everything—including their lives. I vowed I would get my revenge. I tried tae travel through time tae change the outcome of the war, but time wouldnae allow it.

So I went tae the Norse and offered them my help. Nae only will we take back the lands taken from us, we will seize lands from the mainland as well."

Erskina advanced, and Astrid shot out her hand, but before she could issue an Offensive spell, she was rendered still. She realized with horror that Erskina had hurled a Binding spell at both her and Fyfa.

"Ye're tae late tae stop me, Astrid from a time yet tae come," Erskina spat. "I'll grant ye the mercy of death so ye willnae have tae see how ye've failed, and the death and destruction I will bring tae the isles."

With a casual wave of her hand, Astrid's throat began to close. She fought and gasped for breath, but it was as if an invisible hand had closed around her throat, cutting off all air.

The last thing she saw before losing consciousness was Erskina's cold, dark smile.

CHAPTER 21

$\mathcal{A}$strid emerged from a hazy darkness to the feel of strong arms around her, carrying her from the cottage and out into the cool morning air. She opened her eyes as the arms set her down on the ground, meeting Domhnall's panicked blue ones.

"Thank God," he rasped, his eyes filling with emotion. "When I came in and saw ye lying there . . ."

Astrid coughed and reached up to touch her bruised throat where Erskina's spell had taken hold. She surmised that she'd only survived because Erskina must have apparated from the cottage as soon as Astrid passed out, releasing her from the spell's hold.

At the thought of Erskina, the memory of her threats hit Astrid with the force of a sledgehammer, and she sat up.

Behind her, she saw Ruarc helping a dazed-looking Fyfa out of the cottage. Relieved that Fyfa was well, she turned back to face Domhnall, gripping his hands with urgency.

"We need to gather the other witches and lairds to seal the Pact so the alliance can officially begin, and we need to put up every defense we can around the isles. Erskina is powerful, and the Norse have access to that power."

It was nearing sunset as Astrid stood on the islet of Eilean Nan Draoidhean, flanked by Lachina and Fyfa, scanning the horizon for approaching boats.

After Astrid, Domhnall and the others had left Erskina's cottage, they went directly to Lachina, telling her of Erskina's true nature.

Astrid had braced herself for Lachina to not believe her, to hurl angry accusations at her, but Lachina had gone pale and silent before speaking.

"Ever since the war, there's been something dark about Erskina. A simmering rage. She didnae like the outcome of the war; she still has kin who live on Norse lands. I feared the worst she would do would be tae leave our coven tae join her kin. I thought—hoped—time would heal her hatred. I should have sensed her darkness."

Lachina had then sprung into action, calling a meeting with the local coven, dispatching several witches to inform the other coven leaders of what was happening so they could set up magical defenses around the isles, and to have them all come to the islet to seal the Pact by sunset. She'd also dispatched several stiuireadh to accompany Domhnall, Ruarc, and Neacal around the isles to gather the lairds they were allied with. Domhnall would inform their allies of the stiuireadh and the magical alliance they were willing to form, and to warn them of a dark witch working with the Norse.

Once Domhnall and the others had left, Lachina pulled Astrid aside.

"I ken I've been harsh toward ye," she'd said, giving Astrid a look of apology. "Years ago, my sister was killed by an aingidh who wanted her power; I've hated all aingidh ever since. When I detected that yer parents were aingidh, I judged ye for it when I shouldnae have. What ye have warned of has come tae pass. All the while there was a true dark witch in my midst, someone I should have stopped."

"That doesn't matter now," Astrid said, giving her a smile, though relief coursed through her; Lachina's acceptance meant more to her than she'd realized. "All that matters now is sealing the Pact and stopping the Norse from using Erskina's power to claim victory."

Now, she kept her gaze trained on the waters that surrounded the islet, praying that Domhnall had convinced the lairds to ally with the stiuireadh.

Soon she saw boats on the horizon, and relief washed over her. She counted roughly seven approaching, each filled with several men. As they drew near, she spotted Domhnall on the first boat, along with Ruarc and Neacal. A rush of love coursed through her at the sight of him, and the tension ebbed from her body.

When the boats made it to shore and the men scrambled onto shore, Astrid counted twenty-one men, all lairds or nobles by their fine clothing.

Astrid approached Domhnall, who gave her a warm smile that made tingles dance along her skin.

"Was it difficult? Telling them about us and then getting them to agree?"

"Half had already heard of the stiuireadh, others had thought they were myth. When we told them of the Norse working with an aingidh, they were all in agreement about allying with yer kind. It wasnae as hard tae convince them as I'd feared. They all want the same thing—peace for the isles. So much so that they're willing tae align themselves with magic tae achieve it."

Moments later, the lairds and witches all gathered on the shore, the lairds standing opposite the witches in a semicircle. Both Domhnall and Lachina addressed all who were gathered, laying out the terms of the alliance, to which everyone nodded their agreement.

Lachina then turned to face Astrid, gesturing for her to come forward. Astrid hesitated, looking at her in surprise. Since Lachina was the coven leader and had acted as the liaison between the covens, she'd thought Lachina would seal the Pact. As if reading her mind, Lachina said, "As the stiuireadh who has come through time tae make this alliance happen, ye should be the one tae seal the Pact."

Astrid expelled a sharp breath. It was surreal to take part in something she had heard of centuries in the future; it was like being present for the signing of the Declaration of Independence or the Magna Carta. Only this was akin to actually signing one of those vaulted historical documents herself.

This is what you came here for. You were meant to make certain the Pact came about.

She thought of how Fyfa, Siomha and even Domhnall's ally Neacal had foreseen her coming to this time. She was always meant to come here—for this very purpose. It was why her magic wouldn't allow her to turn her back on it, despite her parents' evil.

Time had already written her presence here in the strands of time.

Feeling a sudden sense of calm, Astrid stepped forward. She gestured for everyone to link hands, and once they did, she cited the words of the Pact, first in English, then in Gaelic. Lachina had reviewed the words of the Pact with her, but she also knew it well, having heard it cited in her own time.

"We, the lairds and chieftains of the isles, vow to forever assist the stiuireadh in their quest to protect the strands of time and humanity from those who seek destruction. And we, the stiuireadh of the isles, vow to forever assist the lairds and chieftain of the isles, to protect their lands and people from those who wish them harm."

After both the lairds and the witches finished uttering the words of the Pact, Astrid murmured the words of a Sealing spell, one which would make the Pact into a magical vow, a vow the stiuireadh and lairds would have to heed.

When she finished uttering the spell, she felt cords of magic wind around her, and the others gathered, binding them in a solemn promise, a promise that would forever link the stiuireadh and the lairds of the isles.

A magical Pact that would echo for ages to come.

CHAPTER 22

*A*fter returning to Barra, Domhnall took a ride around the island, accompanied by Astrid, to confirm that his men stationed at various posts were prepared for an offense by sea.

They assured him that they were, the determination and bravery on their faces causing a surge of pride to course through Domhnall. The men of Barra were fierce warriors. They had fought valiantly during the previous war with the Norse. And though he wished it hadn't come to this, he knew they would fight just as valiantly once more.

He and Astrid returned to the castle, where they would share a meal before he joined his men on the ramparts and Astrid joined Lachina and the other witches. They needed a brief reprieve after the tumultuous events of the day.

Astrid went to her chamber to wash and change, and when she returned, she looked lovely in the practical deep green riding gown she'd changed into, the color of the gown bringing out the beauty of her eyes. He drank her in, recalling how beautiful and powerful she'd looked as she'd sealed the Pact, fully in her element as her magic coursed through her. His bonnie sea witch, commanding time and magic to her will.

"We did it, Domhnall," she said, beaming as they sat down to a meal of salted pork and honeyed vegetables, her eyes flushed with excitement. "I can't believe that I was the one who sealed the Pact. It's such an important moment in magical history—most witches in my time know of it. After I turned my back on magic . . ." She trailed off, raw emotion flaring in her eyes. "I never thought such a monumental magical task would fall to me. Now I just have to channel this newfound power into helping destroy Erskina."

Fear swamped him at the thought of her facing off with Erskina again. The dark witch had almost killed Astrid.

"Donnae put yerself in danger," he said. "Let the other witches help ye fight."

"I will," Astrid said, giving him a reassuring smile, "but . . . I feel there's a reason my magic led me to her. I think I'm meant to defeat her."

"Ye're nae here tae cause yerself harm," he growled, that sharp protectiveness seizing him once more.

"Domhnall—"

"I mean it, lass," he said, reaching out to grip her hand. "I ken ye're here tae help, but ye've already united the witches and the lairds. I willnae stop ye from fighting this aingidh, I ken 'tis useless tae do so, but I donnae want ye tae come tae harm, Astrid. I care for ye."

I more than care for ye. As he gazed at her lovely features, the realization struck him hard.

He was in love with his beautiful sea witch.

He'd fantasized before about having her remain in this time. Now, he imagined her in this time not just as his lover, his mistress—but as his wife. His companion. His partner. The mother of his bairns. Lady of Farraige Castle.

He'd never before considered having any other lass permanently by his side. But he'd never teamed up with a lass before as his equal, someone with power of her own. As he took her in, he realized the depth of his love, love he had likely felt for her long before he realized it. He loved her for her compassion, her fierceness, her intelligence, for the power that she used only for good.

Yet she was no ordinary lass. She was a time-traveling witch whose time here was only temporary.

"I'll be careful," Astrid was saying, and unease flitted across her expression as she added, "You too, Domhnall. From what you've told me, I don't believe your cousin will hesitate to kill you."

"I ken," Domhnall said, his gut clenching at the memory of Ulf's ire. "But I'm chieftain and laird. I must protect my people."

"And I'm a time-traveling stiuireadh, bound to

use my magic to help your people," Astrid stubbornly returned. "I suppose we'll both have to be careful."

He couldn't help but smile at her determination. She began to eat, and as he watched her, the woman he loved, he recalled how she'd told him she'd wanted nothing of the past, of time travel, how she wanted to return to her own time, where she had a life. A life without him. There was only light in her eyes when she spoke of the future, this future in which things were better for her. His time didn't hold all the wonders her time offered—only him. And he didn't know if he'd be enough compared to the wonders the future held.

Pain clenched his heart, and he lowered his gaze, trying to focus on his food, which suddenly had no taste. She may not be his forever, but he could savor what little time they had together.

"Do you mind," Astrid said suddenly, "if we talk about something other than the impending battle? I need a moment of respite."

"Aye," he said, realizing how much he needed one as well.

"My uncle would have loved this time," Astrid said with a wistful smile. "He loved horseback riding and the countryside, preferring the quiet to bustling city life. He was the one who taught me to ride; he'd take me to a friend's ranch during the summer."

"I was still a lad when I learned tae ride," he said, a lightness filling him as he recalled the memory: his father's firm words as he guided him, his mother's worried gaze. His parents could have easily had a servant teach him to ride, but they'd insist on doing it themselves.

It was times like these that he realized how much he missed them, and how he was ready to have a family of his own. Pushing away the tempting thought of Astrid as the one he'd start his family with, he listened as Astrid told him about the small town she'd grown up in, raised by her uncle, before moving to the larger city of Los Angeles.

"It's a busy city, so I'd have to find pieces of nature—parks or hiking trails—to find some semblance of peace and quiet," Astrid said, nibbling on a piece of bread.

Domhnall couldn't imagine not being surrounded by nature; it was all he'd known having grown up on Barra.

He suddenly stood, holding out his hand. Astrid took it with a puzzled frown as he led her to the window.

"There is also a place I go tae, somewhere besides the shore outside the castle, when I need peace." He pointed north, toward the distant shadows of bluffs that lined the northern part of the isle. Even though it was dark, he knew every nook and cranny of Barra.

"There's a grove tae the base of that bluff. There's a clearing there that smells of fresh earth, with a small stream that runs through it. Only Ruarc kens about it, and now ye."

He wanted to add that he'd like to take her there, but when? The battle with the Norse and Erskina was looming. Once they hopefully defeated both, she would return to her own time. There would be nothing to keep her here.

"Barra is beautiful," Astrid was saying, taking in the darkened landscape outside the castle. "I'm glad my magic led me here to help you protect it."

"And I'm glad ye came here."

Astrid looked up at him, and unable to stop himself, he leaned down to kiss her. This may be his last time to have her, and he fully intended to take advantage of it.

His love for her coursed through him as their lips melded together, and he lifted her up into his arms, continuing to kiss her as he sat her down on the window's ledge.

"Domhnall," she gasped in surprise, reaching out to steady herself.

"Trust me, lass," he murmured, seizing her lips once more as he slid her gown up her lovely long legs, before kneeling down before her.

She moaned as his tongue dipped into her center, and he kept his eyes locked on her, not wanting to miss a moment of pleasure that danced across her bonnie features. She was sweeter than the most delicious wine, and he moaned against her center as she rubbed herself against him, crying out as her release claimed her. He didn't remove his mouth from her until she stopped quaking.

Only then did he rise, lowering his breeches as he gazed into her green eyes, which were hazy with desire, and sank himself inside her. He would show her how much he needed her; how much he loved her.

"Astrid," he gasped, burying his face in her neck as he thrust inside her, relishing in the feel of her glorious heat around him. Astrid wound her arms around his neck, holding him tight as he buried himself inside her, over and over until she reached another climax and his own release claimed him.

He remained inside her for a long moment, his face still buried in her neck. *I love ye, Astrid. My sea witch.*

He reluctantly stepped back, helping her down from the ledge; he noticed with a possessive ripple of pleasure that her knees slightly wobbled. Her face was still flushed, her lips swollen from his kisses. He took her in, sealing the way she looked now to memory.

She straightened out her gown as Domhnall pulled up his breeches. He studied her, wondering if he was being foolish by not telling her how he felt. What if he fell in battle? He needed her to know his feelings, the depth of his love for her, even though she would soon be gone from his life forever.

"Astrid," he whispered. "I—"

But Astrid's soft gasp made his words die on his lips. She was looking past him out the window, her face ashen. Heart hammering, he turned, following her gaze.

On the horizon, multiple ships were headed their way. Battleships.

Norse ships.

CHAPTER 23

$\mathcal{A}$s Domhnall took in the ships, he realized that the moment he'd dreaded had come. The Norse had launched their invasion. And they had done so at night, likely thinking that Domhnall and his men wouldn't be prepared.

The Norse were very wrong about that.

He turned to face the woman he loved. He needed to get to his men, and she needed to join the witches. But first, he would tell her how he felt.

Now was not the time for fear.

"I love ye, Astrid," he said, his voice raw with emotion. "And after we defeat the Norse, I want ye tae stay by my side. Nae as my mistress, but as my lady. As my wife. As the lass who has captured my heart for her very own." Astrid's eyes widened, and she opened her mouth to speak, but Domhnall interrupted her. "Ye donnae have tae respond—"

"I want to," she returned. "I love you too. When I arrived in this time on that shore and you approached me, I felt as if I already knew you. From the moment I met you, I've felt safe with you. I think I was always meant to love you, just like I was always meant to seal the Pact. I want to stay by your side. You're home to me now, Domhnall."

Joy seized him, momentarily eclipsing his turmoil over the looming battle. He moved toward her, cupping her face, and capturing her mouth with his, pouring all of his love for her, his hope for the future, into their shared kiss. When they parted, Astrid rested her forehead against his.

"Fight well, my love," she whispered.

And before he could say anything more, his bonnie sea witch stepped back, keeping her eyes trained on his, and murmured the words of a spell before disappearing before his eyes.

He stared at the space where she'd stood, aching for her, fearing for her, loving her.

"And ye as well, my Astrid," he murmured.

Now was the time to fight for his lands. For his people.

For a future with the woman he loved.

DOMHNALL MADE his way across the castle ramparts, shouting orders to his men, who scrambled into offensive and defensive positions. The Norse ships were getting even closer to shore, and his men down below had taken up positions all along the shore and around the castle.

"Archers, provide cover for the men down below. But if the Norse approach the castle, unleash your arrows onto them," Domhnall ordered. "And remember—these are yer lands ye fight for."

The men shouted their agreement.

His blood pumping with anticipation, Domhnall turned to make his way off the ramparts as Ruarc joined him.

"Siomha and the other women—they are safe?" he asked.

"Aye," Ruarc said. "I feared Siomha would fight me when I sent her away. But she kent I'd be distracted with worry for her and our babe had she stayed in the castle."

Domhnall had arranged for Siomha and the other women and children who resided in the castle to be sent away for their safety. They were at the manor home of an elderly noble farther inland, where guards were positioned to protect them. Should the worst happen and the Norse breached the castle and made their way inland, the guards were ordered to escort them safely to the mainland; he had boats ready to do so. He could only pray that didn't have to happen.

He and Ruarc made their way down to the shore, joining his men, who stood erect, ready for battle. The conflicting emotions of pride and regret swirled through him. He'd not wanted it to come to this, but he was proud that his men were bravely willing to take a stand once more, so soon after their recent war with the Norse. Determination rose within Domhnall. Tonight, he would fight as hard and as well as he could, to be the leader his men deserved. To be the man his Astrid deserved.

As the enemy ships anchored just off shore and the Norsemen made their way toward Domhnall and his line of men with ferocious roars, the archers above unleashed their arrows and Domhnall shouted for his men to charge.

Domhnall and his men surged forward as one. His sword clashed with the first Norsemen who arrived onshore, their movements frenetic. He managed to knock the man down and turned to face two more, moving quickly to disarm one and fighting off the other.

As he fought man after man, sinking his sword into flesh, knocking men back with his foot and even with the hilt of his sword, he searched the dozens of Norsemen for any sign of his cousin. But he couldn't spot Ulf through the melee, and panic seized him as he realized that the Norse were quickly overpowering his men, making their way past their defensive lines.

"Protect the castle!" he shouted, gesturing for a section of his men to fall back, to assist the guards protecting the castle.

A sword blade whizzed by his head and he ducked and countered, slashing at the Norseman who'd attacked him. As he fought the man, a sudden, heavy fog settled over the shore.

It became even more difficult to see, and

Domhnall realized this was an unnatural fog—one that had appeared suddenly, and it hovered primarily over the defensive line Domhnall's men had formed. Terror gripped him as instinct told him this was a fog caused by magic. Erskina must be near.

Where were the stiuireadh? Lachina had told him they would be near the castle to fend off Erskina should she approach and help with their defenses. Had Erskina harmed or killed them? Killed Astrid?

Grief tore at him at the thought, but he had to keep his focus through the increasingly dense fog, parrying against the various swords that slashed at him. As he continued to fight them off, purely on the defensive now, a man several yards away became visible even in the heavy fog—a man he'd been looking for. His cousin.

Ulf was fighting off Domhnall's men, his eyes trained on Domhnall, moving toward him with deadly purpose. A spear of regret stabbed at his heart, that it had come to this, but he forced himself to push it aside, charging forward toward his cousin with a roar, fighting off Ulf's men as he did so.

His sword met his cousin's with a deafening clash, and they met each other blow for blow. Ulf's blue eyes were shot with fury, and Domhnall realized in horror that his cousin did intend to kill him.

Domhnall landed a successful blow, causing Ulf to stumble back. Now would be the time for a killing blow, but Domhnall couldn't make himself do it. His hesitation cost him as Ulf used it to his advantage, charging forward with a roar, sinking his blade into his stomach.

Pain like he had never known tore through him, sharp and acrid. Stunned, Domhnall collapsed to his knees, feeling his strength ebb from his body. Ulf withdrew his sword, and Domhnall looked up to meet his cousin's eyes. Grief and regret lurked in their depths, and Ulf's eyes filled with tears. As his life bled from him, Domhnall realized dimly that he'd never seen his cousin cry, not even during their fathers' funerals.

"You made me do this, cousin," Ulf spat, his eyes wet with tears. "You did this by betraying your blood."

Too weak to respond, Domhnall fell onto his back as he clutched his stomach, his eyes glazing over as his grief-stricken and enraged cousin held his gaze. Ulf was watching him die.

He closed his eyes, not wanting Ulf's fury and grief to be the last thing he saw before he left this earth. Instead, he allowed his mind's eye to fill with images of his Astrid, her curled up in his arms, her laughter, the feel of her hand in his, her confession of love.

As darkness claimed him, there was a smile on his lips . . . and a sense of peace.

$\mathcal{A}$strid arrived to find Lachina, Fyfa, and two other witches she recognized from the local coven on the shore just south of the castle where they'd agreed to meet. The witches were standing in a semicircle, their hands linked.

Lachina gestured for her to join them, and feeling a sense of kinship with the other witches for the first time, Astrid obliged, joining them and grasping Fyfa's and Lachina's hands.

"We're performing a powerful spell—one that affects the wind," Lachina informed her. "Focus all your energy on commanding the elements. Repeat after me."

Lachina began to chant a spell in Gaelic, and Astrid repeated the spell along with the other witches in a litany.

Astrid didn't recognize the spell; she had never attempted such a powerful spell on her own. She closed her eyes and sent out her request to the natural elements that surrounded them, repeating the words of the spell, over and over, until the words became as familiar to her as her name.

"*Cluinnidh feachdan nàdair ar feachdan gairm nàdur a 'cluinntinn ar tagradh ag iarraidh feachdan gaoithe, gan toirt a-mach.*"

Gradually, the wind picked up around them, responding to their command. Astrid opened her eyes, and though it was dark, she could see two other boats, illuminated by the moonlight, drifting toward the castle—boats that were likely filled with more Norsemen to attack. Astrid poured all of her energy into the spell, imagining that she was propelling the boats away from Domhnall, her love.

"*Cluinnidh feachdan nàdair ar feachdan gairm nàdur a 'cluinntinn ar tagradh ag iarraidh feachdan gaoithe, gan toirt a-mach.*"

She watched in amazement as the boats struggled against the force of the magic-powered winds, which were pushing them back—away from the castle, away from Barra. Eventually, whoever was steering the boats seemed to give up as the boats began to drift in the opposite direction, no longer fighting against the force of the wind.

Elation rose within her at the sight, elation that quickly dissipated, because she felt it again . . . that sense of darkness that only the presence of an aingidh could usher in.

Panicked, she looked at the other witches, and she could tell by their expressions that they could sense it too.

But they kept chanting, giving power to the Wind spell. Astrid looked northward to the castle, and she could see a heavy fog descending, but only on one part of the shore, the part closest to the castle, where Domhnall and his men would be warding off the Norse. And she knew with a chill that magic had conjured that fog. Dark magic.

"Lachina, it's Erskina!" Astrid shouted over the force of the wind. "She's near. I think she's causing that fog!"

"Aye!" Lachina shouted back, her expression grim. "I ken!"

Lachina ordered the witches to keep chanting and moved away from them, murmuring the words of a spell beneath her breath. After a moment, she repeated it again, and Astrid could tell she was getting frustrated.

Astrid broke away from Fyfa and the other witches, instinctively realizing what Lachina was attempting to do—a Searching spell to pinpoint Erskina's exact location.

"Let me try," she said, moving to Lachina's side, praying that Lachina's stubborn pride wouldn't make her refuse. But Lachina said nothing, standing aside and allowing Astrid to hold out her arms, murmuring the words of the Searching spell.

"Thoir an sealladh Erskina thugam."

A shot of darkness seemed to jolt right into her heart, and she stiffened, her eyes landing on one of the boats that hovered just off the shore. Her magic had just shown her Erskina's location.

"She's on that boat!" Astrid shouted. "We need to get to her."

"You and the others stay here. Keep chanting tae keep any other boats away," Lachina said. "I'll Transport myself tae Erskina."

Before Astrid could protest, Lachina was gone.

Astrid bit her lip, uncertainty flaring. She couldn't obey Lachina and stay here . . . something in her gut told her this wasn't Lachina's fight. She was the one who'd unknowingly sensed Erskina the moment she'd arrived in this time; her magic had alerted her to Erskina's presence.

Taking a deep, shuddering breath, she uttered the words of the Transport spell to make herself apparate. There was that dizzying blur of darkness that always claimed her whenever she apparated, and she found herself on a boat.

Adrenaline flooding her veins, she looked around. There were no men on the boat, just Lachina and Erskina, hurling spells at each other.

As soon as Astrid appeared, Erskina's focus turned to her. Her eyes filled with hatred, and she hurled a spell toward her. The force of it tossed Astrid back, slamming her against the side of the boat, sending a fissure of pain down her spine. Erskina stalked toward her, her features taut with fury, opening her mouth to issue a spell. Panic slammed into her chest as some instinct told her it was a Killing spell, and as Erskina shouted the spell—

Lachina hurled herself in front of it, instantly

slumping to the boat's deck as Erskina's spell struck her, her body going eerily still.

Both panic and rage tore through Astrid, and she stumbled to her feet, shouting an Offensive spell that sent Erskina flying through the air, slamming her against the side of the boat. She then shouted a Binding spell, but Erskina dodged it, raising her hand, and once again Astrid found her throat closing.

As she fought for air, Erskina hurled yet another spell at her, sending Astrid's body sailing into the air and over the boat's edge, then plummeting her into the ocean's dark, churning waters.

CHAPTER 25

Astrid sank beneath the waves, fighting to breathe, knowing that it was only a matter of time before death claimed her.

Despair gripped her. She had lost; she would never see Domhnall again.

She thought of all she'd overcome since she'd arrived in this time—her self-doubt, her shame, her denial. She hadn't fought so hard against all of that just to lose to a dark, vengeful witch. With those thoughts, and her love for Domhnall propelling her, Astrid used her waning reserve of strength to silently cast an obscure Flight spell she'd learned from Fyfa—one that Fyfa told her rarely worked. She prayed that it worked now; it was her only hope.

Propel mi suas pro adhair.

Her magic immediately responded to the command of the spell, and she felt the force of her power propelling her body upward, out of the water and onto the deck where she gasped in deep gulps of air.

Once her breathing was steady, she looked around. Erskina was gone, and other than Lachina's still form, the boat was empty, tossing about on the restless waters. Trembling in her wet gown, she crawled toward Lachina, feeling for a pulse. Relief skittered through when she found one; she'd learned during the past few weeks that Killing spells only killed those it was intended for and wounded anyone else, but Lachina had looked frighteningly still.

She pressed her hand to Lachina's chest, uttering a Healing spell. Lachina came to with a startled gasp. She looked around, eyes wild, before her frantic gaze settled on Astrid.

"Erskina?"

"Gone," Astrid said, frustration surging within her. "She almost drowned me and fled."

"I'm tae weak—ye have tae go after her. Ye have a connection with her that I donnae," Lachina said firmly.

Their eyes locked, and for the first time since she met her, Astrid saw trust in her eyes—trust in Astrid.

Astrid gave Lachina a nod and got to her feet, a renewed determination in her heart.

She cast a Transport spell to get herself to shore and looked around. The heavy fog had dissipated, likely because Erskina had been preoccupied with fighting Lachina and Astrid. Around her, illuminated only by moonlight, Domhnall's men fought the Norse, their swords clashing with metallic clangs. She noticed with trepidation that many of Domhnall's men had been beaten back, and the Norse were now storming the castle. A dark chill coiled around her, alerting her to Erskina's presence. She was in the castle.

She turned to head toward the castle, but froze when she spotted a familiar form lying on the beach only several yards away from her.

It was Domhnall. He was lying still, his tunic soaked through with blood.

A strangled sob tore from her throat, and she stumbled toward him. She sank to her knees next to him, grief swelling in her chest. He was ashen and unmoving, and for a moment she was too afraid to reach for his pulse, only to find there wasn't one. But she forced herself to do it, reaching out a trembling hand to press to the side of his neck.

Relief flooded her like a tsunami at the feel of a pulse; it was there, but weak. But she had to think quickly. Just because he was alive now didn't mean he would stay that way; he'd lost a great deal of blood.

It was time to put both her medical and her magical knowledge to use. She reached down to her wet gown and tore the very bottom of it off, using it as a tourniquet to wrap around his abdominal area to staunch his bleeding. She mentally reviewed every Healing spell she knew until she thought of the best ones, and pressed her hands to his abdomen, not caring how much this drained her of her magic. Keeping Domhnall alive was more important to her than stopping Erskina, than even her own life.

"*Slànaich lotan an duine seo, cuir air ais am fuil.*"

Domhnall didn't stir, and panic rippled through her. Was she too late? Had he already lost too much blood?

"Domhnall!" she shouted, over the sound of clashing swords, roaring wind, and churning ocean waves. "I love you. I love you, and you're going to live. Do you understand me?"

Tears stinging her eyes, she poured every ounce of her energy, of her love, into the Healing spells, uttering them over and over until her voice was hoarse.

But he remained still.

Astrid let out a sob, resting her head on his chest. Despair and anguish seized her; she couldn't have traveled back centuries in time to find the love of her life only to lose him.

Through her tears, she felt a hand on her hair. Assuming it was one of Domhnall's men, she pushed it away, but stilled.

Because the hand belonged to Domhnall.

She looked up, tears blinding her eyes as she met Domhnall's blue ones. He looked dazed and out of sorts, but he was alive, and looking at her with such love.

"Domhnall," Astrid gasped, and not caring that

they were on the edge of a raging battlefield, she leaned down to kiss him, a kiss that he returned.

When they broke apart, he briefly rested his forehead on hers. "Ye saved my life," he rasped, looking at her with awe as she helped him sit up. "How?"

"Healing spells," she said.

As she spoke, she realized how weak she felt. But now that Domhnall had been revived, she still needed to find and destroy Erskina. "I have to find Erskina—she's inside the castle. You need to find somewhere safe to rest and—"

"Ye've healed me," Domhnall said, giving her a stubborn scowl. "I'm the leader of these men. I will fight until this battle is won."

Astrid studied the man she loved, wanting to argue with him, but it was no use; she knew he wouldn't budge on this. And her Healing spell had taken care of his abdominal wound. He may be slightly weaker now, but he was still capable of fighting.

"Just—don't get yourself stabbed again," she said, helping him up, going for a bit of levity though she was terrified. She'd never forget the torrential grief that had claimed her during those brief moments when she'd thought he was dead.

He gave her a grim smile, his hand going to the hilt of his sword. He reached for her hand, and together they made their way into the castle.

As soon as they entered, Astrid smelled something burning coming from the great hall, and heard the sounds of swords clashing coming from the rear courtyard.

Dread encircled her; Erskina was trying to burn down the castle. "Erskina's in the great hall— I'm going to stop her," Astrid said, determination swelling in her once more.

"I'm going tae join my men."

He took her hand and lifted it to his lips, giving her a searing look that said so much before darting toward the rear courtyard.

Heart pounding, Astrid made her way to the great hall. Erskina was inside, her hands raised, watching with pleasure as the fires from the fireplace swelled, threatening to encase the entire hall.

Astrid shouted an Extinguishing spell, killing the fires, and Erskina whirled, her eyes widening in disbelief and rage.

"Ye donnae stay dead," she hissed, stalking toward Astrid.

She began to hurl Killing spells at Astrid, one after the other, forcing Astrid to use a Cloaking spell to shield herself, something that drained her already weakened power reserves.

It was then that she realized what Erskina was doing. She must have realized Astrid was weakened; all she had to do was tire Astrid out with Offensive spells until she could deliver the killing blow.

Panic coursed through Astrid as she continued to dodge each spell and counteract with weak

Offensive ones of her own, spells which Erskina easily dodged.

Astrid had to think fast. She recalled how her fear had helped her issue a powerful spell when she'd first arrived in this time against Domhnall, when he hadn't believed that she was a witch. Fear had hindered her for her entire life, ever since the dark days of her childhood. But now she could use fear to save her life, to propel the last of her energy into a powerful spell that would destroy this dark witch for good.

Astrid cleared her mind, meeting Erskina's fury-filled eyes, and then she did something that seemed counterintuitive on the surface.

She turned and ran.

Erskina was instantly on her heels, laughing with dark delight at what she perceived to be Astrid's cowardice. Astrid kept running, her heart in her throat, praying that her hastily put together plan would work.

Once they were safely outside the castle, Astrid whirled to face Erskina. As Erskina opened her mouth to shout another Killing spell, Astrid raised her hand, funneling every last remnant of her power into a Fire spell.

A blazing ring of fire surrounded Erskina, trapping her. Her eyes widened in horror as Astrid shouted another spell, a spell she'd never hoped to utter in her lifetime.

"Marbh an stiuireadh seo."

Astrid made herself hold Erskina's gaze as the

Killing spell struck her, watching as a multitude of emotions filled her eyes—rage, regret, grief, until the life drained from them, and she slumped to the ground, dead.

Only then did Astrid extinguish the fire, looking down at Erskina's still body with sorrow. In some ways, Erskina reminded her of her parents, choosing darkness that would ultimately twist her soul and lead to her downfall.

I'm sorry, Astrid thought, gazing down at the fallen witch. *But you picked the wrong path. You chose darkness, and this is where it led you.*

A peace fell over her, and for the first time, she was truly able to let go of the dark legacy her parents' long-ago actions had cast over her. Erskina and her parents had chosen darkness. Astrid had chosen a different path, one of light; it was a path which led her to love, to Domhnall.

It was the one she would always follow.

GIVEN how weak Astrid was after the power and multitude of her spells had drained her, she barely made it to the rear courtyard, having to grip the wall to hold herself upright.

When she arrived, remaining in the safety of the castle's rear doorway to stay out of the fray of battle, she saw that the fighting had mostly died down; Domhnall's men had clearly turned the tide of battle in their favor. There were men scattered about the courtyard, either injured or dead, and Domhnall's men were taking away Norsemen as prisoners.

Still, a handful of men continued to fight, including Domhnall and a tall, blond man she knew from Domhnall's description was his cousin, Ulf.

She wanted to come to Domhnall's aid, but her magical reserves were empty; she could barely hold herself upright. She could only watch, helpless, as Domhnall and Ulf fought, moving in a series of rapid-fire sword clashes. It was hard to believe that Domhnall had been near death when she found him on the shore; her spell had indeed restored him.

She noticed that Ulf's movements seemed to be fueled by rage. Domhnall was more calculated, and she realized that Domhnall was counting on Ulf's unrestrained, impulsive moves.

Soon Ulf made a fatal mistake, jabbing his sword forward as Domhnall dodged. Domhnall was able to knock the sword from Ulf's hands, kicking him to the ground with his foot. Ulf landed hard on his back, but glared up at his cousin with defiance.

"Do it, traitor," Ulf hissed. "Kill me."

Domhnall held his blade above his cousin's chest, his torment evident. After several long moments, Domhnall slowly lowered it, stepping back, and gesturing for two of his hovering men to come forward to restrain Ulf.

"There has been enough death," Domhnall

said. "Yer men have lost. I willnae become like ye and allow rage tae consume me."

Domhnall nodded to his men, who took away a furious-looking Ulf.

Relief flowed through her just as Domhnall turned, meeting her eyes. She gave him a wavering smile, but her weakness claimed her, and her legs gave way.

To her surprise, she didn't fully lose consciousness. Instead, the world around her went blurry, and she felt strong arms around her, holding her up. In medical terms, it felt as if she'd had a stroke, but she was too weak to feel panic.

Around her, there were the sounds of muffled voices, and gradually, her strength returned, her vision becoming clear once more.

She blinked, looking up. Domhnall had her in his arms, his pale features stark with relief. Fyfa hovered at his side, giving her a warm smile.

"Lachina told me tae come tae yer aid, but I saw ye'd already destroyed Erskina. The least I could do was restore yer strength. I used a Healing spell on ye, but ye should still rest."

"I thank ye, Fyfa," Domhnall said, giving her a grateful smile.

Fyfa returned his smile and nodded, reaching out to squeeze Astrid's hand before moving into the courtyard, approaching a group of injured nobles.

Astrid turned her focus to Domhnall, who cupped her face. "My bonnie, brave Astrid," he murmured. "Ye frightened me."

"My magic just drained me," she reassured him. "Is the battle over?"

"Aye. My men have fought back the Norse on Barra. I will join Neacal shortly tae confirm his men have staved them off as well, and then we will check with our allies on the other isles. It seems Erskina was the only aingidh working with the Norse."

Relief filled Astrid, and she closed her eyes. It was hard to believe it was all over, but the peace that had settled over her confirmed it.

Domhnall lifted her up into his arms, ignoring her insistence that she could walk, taking her to his chamber, and setting her down on her bed.

"This will be yer chamber from now on," he said, giving her a searching, hopeful look, "if ye choose tae stay in this time. If ye choose tae be my bride."

He waited for her response, his handsome face raw and vulnerable as if he expected her to refuse.

She smiled, reaching up to touch his face. "You foolish man," she whispered. "Didn't I tell you that my home is with you?"

Joy infused his features, and he leaned forward to capture her lips with his. She wrapped her arms around him, clinging to him, relishing in the sense of happiness and contentment that had settled over her, a contentment that had evaded her until now. Until this very moment.

"I love you, Laird Domhnall Flachnan," she whispered.

"And I love ye, Lady Astrid Flachnan," he returned, his voice husky with reverence. Her heart swelled at hearing her future title—a title she was always meant to have. "My bonnie love from the future. And now, ye are my future. My verrae heart."

EPILOGUE

One Month Later

Astrid and Domhnall were married on the same shoreline she'd arrived at when she'd first come to this time.

It was an unusual place to have a wedding in this time period, especially for a laird, whose weddings usually took place in the great hall of his castle or manor. But Domhnall happily agreed to wed there when Astrid suggested it. It was where they'd first found each other in the vast fabric of time, sealing their place in each other's lives.

The lairds and witches who'd taken part in the Pact were in attendance, including Fyfa and Lachina, who looked on at the happy couple with warm smiles on their faces. Astrid had officially joined the local coven two weeks after they'd helped defeat the Norse; her fellow witches now welcomed her with open arms.

Astrid had spent the last few weeks before wedding Domhnall getting adjusted to living permanently in this time. In addition to her position as the lady of Farraige Castle, she was now the castle healer. Her first task was assisting with Siomha's labor; she had given birth to a baby girl. Despite being born a few weeks early, the wee lass, who Ruarc and Siomha had named Innis, was healthy and strong.

Astrid relished in using her medical knowledge from the future to help heal ailments in this time, from minor scrapes and bruises to more serious infections. She was also growing in power and confidence with her magic, often using magic in conjunction with her medical skills.

Domhnall had confirmed with Neacal and their other allies that they, with the help of the stiuireadh, had warded off the Norse invasion with minimal losses of their own. The lairds of the isles had come to a new peace agreement with the Norse, who officially ceded their claims to the Scottish isles, agreeing to not attack them again. It seemed they too were now weary of warfare; it had taken a toll.

Barra and the other Scottish isles finally had peace.

His cousin Ulf remained imprisoned, and though he remained stubbornly silent whenever Domhnall visited, he had noticed the corners of Ulf's mouth twitch with a hint of a smile when Domhnall told him he was to wed.

Though Ruarc and his men didn't like that Domhnall had spared Ulf, Domhnall was glad that he had. Guilt would have shadowed him had he not, and after much warfare and finding love with Astrid, he wanted a clear heart. Ulf was kin, and he loved him; he'd never forget the grief in Ulf's eyes when Ulf had thought he'd killed him.

And he could see by the wariness in Ulf's eyes that he no longer had any desire to fight, especially when Domhnall told him of the new peace agreement he and his allies had made with the Norse. Rather than looking angered by this, relief had flickered across his expression.

As Domhnall walked away from Ulf the last time he'd visited, his cousin's voice stopped him in his tracks; it was the first time Ulf had spoken since Domhnall had imprisoned him.

"I'm glad," Ulf said gruffly, not looking at him, "that you survived my attack. I—I couldn't have lived with myself had you died. I've had much time in here to think. No land was worth your death, cousin."

Domhnall studied his cousin for a long moment. "And I'm glad I spared ye. We are blood, cousin. I only want peace going forward."

Ulf gave him a hint of a smile, which Domhnall returned before leaving. Domhnall could see them one day repairing their fractured relationship, and being able to release Ulf from his custody, something that filled him with great relief.

Now Domhnall kissed his new bride, joy

flooding him, a joy that remained throughout their celebratory feast in the great hall, and then as his men cheered as he carried his new bride to their chamber.

Astrid had told him of a tradition in her time in which the man carried his bride over the threshold; it was something he was eager to do.

He kept his eyes pinned on his new bride as he carried her over the threshold of their chamber. She looked sinful in her wedding gown of emerald green, her hair loose and flowing about her shoulders at his request.

"Tonight," he rasped, setting down the love of his life on to their bed, "we begin our family. I want tae plant a bairn in yer belly, wife. The first of many."

"I want that too," Astrid said, beaming up at him as she reached out to stroke his face. "I can't wait to start a family with you. A life with you. You are what I've been missing, Domhnall. I didn't know it until I met you."

He kissed her, her words searing on to his very soul. She was the missing piece in his life as well, a life that was now whole. "I love ye, my Astrid. Ye're home now."

Astrid's eyes filled with emotion as they kissed, and he proceeded to show her just how much he loved her . . . how much he would always love his bonnie witch from the sea, from a time yet to come, who had made his life whole.

ON THE SHORE across from Farraige Castle, two stiuireadh watched as the candlelight in Laird Flachnan's chamber went out.

With their knowledge of the future, Siobhan and Lioslaith knew that tonight Astrid and Domhnall would conceive a son, the first of four healthy bairns the two would have.

As Astrid's coven leader, Siobhan had worried about Astrid when she'd first gone to the past, knowing of her destiny here. She was fearful that Astrid would refuse to undertake the task the threads of time had bestowed upon her.

But she had undertaken it with gusto, uniting with her fated partner in the past, Domhnall, and bringing about peace. Together, Domhnall and Astrid made each other whole; time had stitched their paths together.

Siobhan turned to Lioslaith, who stood at her side, beaming at the darkened window. Lioslaith, who was a powerful fiosaiche, was aware of the ripple effects of Astrid's presence here, of the other witches who would come to the past to help the lairds maintain peace.

"All is well," Lioslaith said in her musical voice, meeting Siobhan's eyes with a smile.

Siobhan nodded, reaching for Lioslaith's hand. It was time for them to return to their respective times, to ensure that the stiuireadh and other travelers destined to pass through the fabric of time made it to their various destinations.

Every once in a while, they liked to travel to the past to see the effects of a time traveler's journey—love found, peace restored.

They'd seen it here with Astrid and Domhnall.

Giving the darkened chamber window one last look, Siobhan returned Lioslaith's smile.

"All is well."

GLOSSARY

Below please find a glossary of magical terms used in the novel.

aingidh - a stiuireadh who uses magic for dark purposes

fiosaiche - Seers who can detect anomalies in the flow of time

Pact - the agreement between the stiuireadh and the chieftains of the Scottish isles pledging to assist the stiuireadh in times of need

Sight - the ability to see glimpses or visions of the future

Seer - see *fiosaiche* above

sidhe - a term for fairies in Scottish and Irish mythology

stiuireadh - a witch or witches who possess the ability to travel through time

ACKNOWLEDGMENTS

Another series complete, another group of fabulous people to thank!

First of all, I'd like to thank the amazing and talented Kim Killion for her design of the lovely covers for the Highlander Fate, Lairds of the Isles series. It was a hard job looking through stock photos of hot kilted men for the covers, and Kim made it a blast.

Secondly, my amazing editor Paula, whose patience, thoroughness and professionalism is more than any writer could ask for.

Thirdly, my amazing husband-best friend-snuggler-hot-Highlander inspiration, Mr. Knight. I've said it before and I'll say it again, you make writing dreamy heroes a cinch.

And of course, a sincere thanks to my dear, dear readers, from my advance readers to my newsletter subscribers to any and all who have read any of my books. Thank you, thank you, thank you. Your words of praise in the form of reviews, private messages and even Facebook comments make my day. You make it possible for me to have the best job in the world.

Thank you for being such awesome readers.

ABOUT THE AUTHOR

Stella Knight writes time travel romance and historical romance novels. She enjoys transporting readers to different times and places with vivid, nuanced heroes and heroines.

Stay in touch!
stellaknightbooks.com
stella@stellaknightbooks.com